"Is that a challenge?"

For a long moment he stared down into her eyes.

She cursed herself for the tears spilling and slipping down her cheeks. The moisture stung as the subzero air froze the liquid in place.

Sam pulled her hard against him.

Kat didn't protest. She let him hold her like she had wanted to be held.

His mouth descended over hers and he kissed her. Long and hard, she sank deeper and deeper into him until she couldn't remember where she ended and Sam began.

Heat built inside her, pooling in the pit of her belly, spreading lower. She wanted more.

She could have stood there forever in the warmth and protection of Sam's arms.

The sharp crack of gunfire pulled them apart.

ELLE JAMES

ALASKAN FANTASY

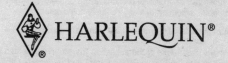

HARLEQUIN®

TORONTO • NEW YORK • LONDON
AMSTERDAM • PARIS • SYDNEY • HAMBURG
STOCKHOLM • ATHENS • TOKYO • MILAN • MADRID
PRAGUE • WARSAW • BUDAPEST • AUCKLAND

I dedicate this book to the many adventurers who
participate in the Iditarod race, and specifically to Paul
and Evy Gebhardt. These wonderful people took the time
to read through this manuscript to make sure I got the
details correct on the terrain and equipment. I'd also like
to thank my cousin Victor Hughes and his lovely wife,
Nancy, who love dogsledding, the dogs and Alaska so
much they inspired me to write this story.

ISBN-13: 978-0-373-69300-9
ISBN-10:   0-373-69300-1

ALASKAN FANTASY

www.eHarlequin.com

Printed in U.S.A.

ABOUT THE AUTHOR

A 2004 Golden Heart Award winner for Best Paranormal Romance, Elle James started writing when her sister issued the Y2K challenge to write a romance novel. She managed a full-time job, raised three wonderful children and she and her husband even tried their hands at ranching exotic birds (ostriches, emus and rheas) in the Texas hill country. Ask her, and she'll tell you, what it's like to go toe-to-toe with an angry 350-pound bird! After leaving her successful career in information technology management, Elle is now pursuing her writing full-time. She loves building exciting stories about heroes, heroines, romance and passion. Elle loves to hear from fans. You can contact her at ellejames@earthlink.net or visit her Web site at www.ellejames.com.

Books by Elle James

CAST OF CHARACTERS

Sam Russell—Geologist targeted for sabotage. Is it because of his chance to win the Iditarod, or for what he knows about the interior oil fields of Alaska?

Katherine "Kat" Sikes—Stealth Operations specialist who lost her husband to an explosion and came back to Alaska to forget.

James Blalock—Alaskan senator bent on developing Alaska's interior.

Al Fendley—Hunting outfitter and race competitor. Does he have more at stake than just the race?

Warren Fendley—Al's business partner, he will do anything to see his brother succeed.

Vic Hughes—Alaskan native who knows the terrain, the competitors and the dogs.

Nicole "Tazer" Steele—Stealth Operations specialist assigned to help Kat find Sam's saboteur.

Paul Jenkins—Kat's brother, barred from the race after sled sabotage led to a broken ankle.

Chapter One

Snow glittered like a million scattered diamonds in the light cast by the fat, gold moon hovering low on the horizon. Winter in Alaska may be filled with dark days, but its nights were no less beautiful than summer. Silence reigned, broken only by the crackle of the sled runners and the patter of sixteen sets of paws skimming across the icy crust.

Sam Russell tugged the wool scarf down off the lower half of his face and breathed in the frigid, clean air. The moisture in his breath crystallized as it left his mouth. After living in the frozen North for the past four years, he couldn't imagine returning to the the lower forty-eight states with their noise, traffic and pollution.

His broken engagement and his career change were the best things to ever happen to him. He couldn't picture his ex-fiancée, Leanne, braving freezing temperatures or enjoying the solitude. She'd have gone stark raving mad without the shopping malls and soirees of her busy social life.

A shiver coursed down his spine and he replaced the scarf over his nose and mouth.

The sight of another sled in the clearing ahead reminded Sam he wasn't completely alone. Not that he minded Paul Jenkins. Paul was one of the few friends he'd made in his time here.

Although he caught glimpses of Paul through the branches of the spruce trees and lodgepole pine, the trail veered sharply to the right, skirting a jumble of fallen logs crisscrossing the forest floor. Sam leaned to the right and shouted, "Gee!" to lead dogs Hammer and Striker. They turned down the path, the other fourteen dogs following, pulling hard in the traces. The long line of dogs dipped down into a frozen creek bed and back up on the other side.

When the sled hit the bottom of the creek, the runners slammed against a rock hidden beneath the snow and lurched to the right. Sam bent his knees, absorbing the jolt, then compensated for the listing sled by leaning left. The dogs pressed forward, driven by the need to run.

When canines and sled topped the creek bank, the trail opened to the clearing nestled in the pine forest where Paul awaited them. The team sent up a chorus of yelps, their excitement over meeting with others of their kind apparent in the added bounce in their step and the frantic tail wagging.

"Whoa!" Sam stepped on the foot brake and anchored the snow hook in the powder, bringing the dogs to a halt beside Paul and his sled. Hammer and Striker flopped down on the snow, barely breathing hard, their ears perked in anticipation of Sam's next command.

"About time you showed up." Paul strode toward him, his boots sinking into snow up to his knees. He pulled his goggles down around his neck and smiled. The man always had an infectious grin, as if he saw something funny in every situation. Paul loved his life in Alaska and wanted everyone to love it right along with him. "Any problems?"

Sam tugged his goggles up on his forehead. "I hit a rock in the creek bottom."

Dark brows angled down over light blue eyes as Paul shot a glance toward Sam's sled. "Any damage?"

"It handled beautifully." He climbed from the runners and sank into the snow.

Paul's frown cleared. "So, how do you like the new sled?"

"So far so good." The sled had arrived two weeks ago and he'd been working with it ever since, testing it thorughly before he decided whether or not to use it on the Iditarod. It had to be good to make it in the eleven-hundred-mile race from Anchorage to Nome.

"I've been thinking about investing in a new one myself." Paul scratched at the week-old beard on his chin. "But I'm kinda attached to the one I used last year."

Sam waved a hand toward his sled and team of dogs. "Want to try it out?"

Paul's eyes sparkled. "Do you mind?"

"Not at all." Sam stepped away from the sled. "Did you plan to take them any farther today?"

"No. I didn't want to work the team too hard with the race only two days away. I'm ready to head back and start packing, if you are."

"Yeah. I hadn't planned on going more than ten miles today. Had to replace Jonesy with Trooper and wanted to see how the team reacted to the placement."

"What happened to Jonesy?" Paul knew all the dogs in the shared kennel and cared as much as Sam or Vic about their well-being, not just because of their importance to the race. They were part of the family.

"Vic said Jonesy was favoring his left shoulder. I didn't want to chance it with him."

Paul nodded. "Not with the race so close."

"Tell you what." Sam waved at his sled and team. "Why don't you take my sled back to the house."

"No need. I'll just take it a couple miles to get the feel for it. Don't want to confuse the dogs with a different musher."

Sam snorted. "They're more used to you than me. You're the one who feeds and trains them year-round. I only show up during the wintertime."

"Yeah, but what I wouldn't give for the fun job you do. The Anchorage police force isn't nearly as thrilling as tramping through the woods discovering the next great oil field in the interior."

Sam had to admit he liked being out in the wild, although sometimes it was lonely. "It's not as exciting as you make it sound. It's got its drawbacks. Mainly the politics."

"Oh, come on. Don't make me laugh. I'd trade places

with you in a heartbeat to get out in the woods more often." Paul shrugged. "But I know what you mean. We have our own share of politics in the police force, but nothing like what you're dealing with."

"Maybe I'll take you up on that trade. Tramping through the wild with nothing more substantial than an ATV can be hair-raising at times. Especially when you come face-to-face with a grizzly. Although, I think I'd rather face a grizzly than the congressional committees of the White House, any day."

Paul grinned. "Same here. And I'd rather face a grizzly than a moose. I once stood completely still for two hours waiting for a two-thousand-pound bull moose to finish grazing and move off the trail so I could get by. That damn moose really bit into my finish time on the Yukon Quest. Ended up in fourth place that year."

"Out of how many entrants?" Sam asked.

"Fifty."

Sam grinned, shaking his head. "I'm not feeling sorry for you."

Paul laughed out loud. "I was pretty proud of my placement. Never got that close before. I'm really looking forward to this race."

"I think you have a shot at the top ten this year."

"So do you, my friend," Paul said.

"I've only been at it for the past three years, I'm glad just to participate. I wouldn't even have considered it without you and Vic leading me by the hand." Sixty-eight entrants were preparing for the race to begin that Saturday, the first weekend of March. Sam still couldn't believe he was going to run in one of the world's most famous dogsled races.

"Yeah, thank God for Vic." Paul pulled his goggles back up over his eyes. "He taught me and Kat everything we know about sledding."

"Speaking of your sister, isn't she getting in today? I'm surprised you're out here running the dogs when she hasn't been home in a year."

"She insisted on Vic picking her up at the airport. She knows this close to the race the dogs need to exercise regularly. Her plane got in around five, so she should be at the house by the time we get back."

"Then we better get going." Sam shifted the brake and walked to the front of his team. As he passed by, the dogs hopped to their feet, tails wagging, ready to resume the run. Sam reached out, patting heads and checking necklines and ganglines along the way. When he reached Striker and Hammer, he knelt and scratched behind the two dogs' ears. "Ready for another run, boys?"

Hammer jumped up in Sam's face, planting a long wet tongue across his cheek.

Sam laughed and wiped away the quickly freezing moisture with the back of his gloved hand. "Line out." Striker immediately leaned forward in his traces, stretching the length of the tethered team. He kicked up snow and dirt with his back feet like a bull facing a matador, as if reminding the rest of the team he was boss. Hammer was a little slower in the effort, but leaned into his harness next to Striker.

"You teamed them well," Paul said. "Striker's the

strongest and smartest, but, Hammer has the desire to stay the head of the pack."

Striker stood still, his brown-black eyes peering intently down his pale red snout. He wouldn't jump up in Sam's face unless directed to do so. Striker was the serious, patient lead, chosen for his intelligence and stamina. And in the pecking order among the pack, he was top dog. Even Hammer didn't cross him without retribution.

"Good dog." Sam ruffled Striker's neck and, grabbing the dog's harness, he led the team in a sweeping circle, turning them to face the direction they'd come.

Paul performed the same task with his team, then strode over to Sam's sled. "Ready to go? I want to see how this baby flies."

"You'll like it." Sam grabbed the handlebar of Paul's sled and prepared to follow his friend out of the clearing and back to Paul's home, where he stayed during the winter months.

Paul clicked his tongue and the dogs shot forward and down into the creek bed. Heading home, they stretched out and ran like the wind.

Sam waited until they cleared the creek bed and then shouted, "Let's go!" Paul's team strained against the harnesses as Sam pedaled one foot in the snow until the sled was moving fast enough for him to hop aboard. Down into the creek and back up, they maintained a two-hundred-yard distance behind Paul on the new sled.

The trail wound along the base of a mountain and through the woods, curving with the steep banks of a river.

Sam sank back into the trance of solitude he'd achieved on the trek out. His mind drifted over the snow, erasing all his cares in the wake of the powder stirred up by his runners. This was the life he was meant to lead. No pretense, no corporate clowns calling the shots. Just him, the dogs and hundreds of miles of snow and silence.

Beat the hell out of the shouting matches he had to look forward to in the congressional committee meeting he was due to attend two weeks after the race. The Alaskan senator, James Blalock, wouldn't listen to him when he'd warned that the initial oil samples weren't of a grade sufficient to warrant drilling. With all the stink over disturbing the natural order of the Alaskan interior, he thought Blalock would be happy. Sam shook his head. Who knew what the senator was thinking.

Ahead, Paul raced around a sharp bend in the river on the right and disappeared behind a hill to his left.

Twenty yards from the curve in the trail, the silence was shattered by the sound of dogs yelping. Not the excited yelp of running a race, but the kind of barking they used when hurt or frightened. Sam's heart slammed against his rib cage. What happened? The dogs had been on this path before, they knew the way. Had a moose stepped into the trail?

His team leaped forward without Sam having to encourage them, as if they were just as worried about the other dogs as Sam was about Paul.

When he rounded the corner on the narrow strip of land between the base of the hill and the river below, he didn't see the sled or the dogs. But the yelping continued. Then he saw the runner marks in the snow leading over the ledge of the steep riverbank.

"Whoa!" Sam hit the brake and jammed the hook into the snow, bringing the team to a halt. He leaped off the sled and stared down the embankment toward the frozen river.

The sled lay sideways on the chunky ice fifteen feet below. Sixteen dogs struggled against their tangled ganglines only making the mess worse. Paul was nowhere to be seen.

"Stay!" Sam shouted to the team on the trail and he scrambled down the riverbank to the snow-covered ice below.

When he reached the sled, he clambered to the other side. There on the cold, hard surface of the river lay Paul, as still as death.

"THANKS FOR PICKING us up, Vic," Kat Sikes said quietly as the truck ate the miles between Anchorage International Airport and the house nestled in the breathtaking mountains surrounding the city. The ragged peaks were outlined against the starlit night sky, calling to her, welcoming her home.

"I wouldn't have missed you for the world. We don't get to see you very often." He reached across and squeezed her hand. Vic Hughes had been as happy as a little kid to see her step through the security gate. He'd practically crushed every bone in her body hugging her.

Her friend, Nicole "Tazer" Steele had been treated to the same bone-crunching hug as Kat. Unlike Kat's curly mop flying every which way, Tazer's shoulder-length, straight blond hair fell back in place leaving her looking like a model poised to step onto the runway. Beneath the blond beauty's feminine looks was a core of steel. Unarmed, she could drop a two-hundred-fifty-pound man to his knees in seconds. Kat had seen it happen. Thus Nicole had earned her team nickname of Tazer. No one called her Nicole.

Tazer insisted on sitting quietly in the backseat of the SUV. Kat sat up front with Vic. She loved Vic like the father she and Paul lost when they were still in their teens. Vic was the only family they had left in Alaska, a distant cousin, but family nonetheless. Kat struggled to suppress the quick rise of tears. She'd missed Vic and Paul, the dogs and…well, everything about home. Taking a deep breath, she asked, "How are the preparations for the race?"

"Paul and Sam are out exercising the dogs. You should ask them. Paul's really excited about his team this year. He thinks he might have a chance to win. And Sam won't do so badly, either. His team's looking really strong."

"Is Sam the boarder Paul took in?"

"Sure is." Vic shot a grin her way. "Nice guy. You're gonna love him."

Kat still wasn't sure whether or not she liked the idea of someone besides family living in their home. Not that she'd been there in over a year. After her husband, Marty, died, she'd felt a distinct tug of jealousy and homesickness that Paul had a friend to keep him company in their family home and all she had was her lonely apartment in D.C.

It had been a year since Marty was killed on an assignment at the embassy in the small African nation of Dindi. A year of loneliness and drifting from one operation to the next, barely able to focus on the mission at hand. Her boss finally insisted she get away and "pull herself together."

At first she'd resented his inference that she was falling apart. Forced into taking leave, she headed to the only place she knew Marty had never been. It still struck her as ironic that Marty had never seen her home. Paul had always come out to visit them and, with their jobs being so demanding and dangerous, they never got around to doing anything other than brief trips into the North Carolina mountains to bike or backpack. They'd both been dedicated to their jobs and loved the thrill of being Stealth Operations Specialists—ultra-secret agents. But after Marty's death…

"Is that your house?" Tazer leaned over the back of the seat, staring ahead.

The two-story log cabin perched on the side of a hill, the roof banked in a foot of snow, warm yellow light streaming through every window. Kat's heart lodged in her throat and tears burned behind her eyelids. She would not cry. Having been raised in a malecentric household, tears were considered worse than the plague. On top of her upbringing, she'd spent time in the army as a criminal investigator and in Washington, D.C., on the Capitol police force before she was recruited to be an S.O.S. agent. Everywhere she'd been tears were taboo.

Kat wasn't a woman prone to waterworks. At first

she'd been glad Tazer had asked to go along with her to Alaska, but now she wished her friend was back in D.C. The homecoming would be twice as hard if she had to wear a game face all the time.

Vic pulled up in the driveway and all three climbed out of the SUV. "I'll take your luggage in. Loki is around back. He'll be glad to see you."

"Loki?" Tazer pulled her collar up around her neck, hunching her shoulders against the frigid breeze.

Kat's tears pushed closer to the surface as she managed to choke out, "My lead dog."

"If you don't mind, I'd like to go in and climb into a cup of really hot coffee." Tazer stamped her feet in the snow.

"No, please. Vic will show you to your room. I'll join you for coffee in a few." Kat took off around the side of the house, knowing if she didn't, she'd break down in front of Tazer.

As she approached the rows of doghouses, a light sensor triggered the outside flood lamp and a familiar, furry face lifted from his paws. As soon as Loki saw her, he leaped to his feet and barked, his body twisting and shaking in his excitement.

Kat dropped to her knees before the Alaskan husky launched himself into her arms, licking her face and whining at the same time.

Swallowing past the lump in her throat, Kat couldn't hold back any longer. She wrapped her arms around Loki's neck, buried her face in his thick black-and-white fur and let the past year wash over her in a tsunami of emotions.

Visions of Marty laughing among the group at the S.O.S. office in D.C., Marty on their wedding day when they'd flown to Atlantic City to get married, and the last time she'd seen him alive as he boarded the plane to Dindi. He'd kissed her goodbye and tapped her beneath the chin. "See ya in a few."

The only time he'd ever mentioned the L-word had been when he'd promised to love, honor and cherish her until death do us part. And death had parted them only a year after their whirlwind courtship and marriage. Sometimes Kat wondered if they really had been married. A year in the life of an S.O.S. agent was short. With the dangerous work they did, flying all over the world, they'd barely seen each other.

She'd loved him hard, as if each day would be the last. And she felt the pain of his loss no less than if they'd been married fifty years. But she'd learned one thing. Love hurt too much to invest in a second time. "Oh, Loki, it's so good to be home."

"Hey!" A voice called out from somewhere down the hill at the rear of the house. "Hey! Help!"

Kat's head jerked up and she scrubbed the tears from her eyes before she could see a team of dogs and a sled in the moonlight coming across the clearing behind the house. The team was twice as long as the usual team. The sled had a large lump sprawled across it, and a man with a voice she didn't recognize behind it.

From across the clearing, the man yelled, "Call an ambulance! Paul's hurt!"

Chapter Two

Sam leaned against the wall of the crisp, clean hospital room, awaiting his chance to speak to Paul alone.

Kat leaned over her brother and pressed a kiss to his cheek. Her dark hair slid across his chest in a cloud of ebony waves. "I'm going to get some coffee." Kat tucked the blanket up around Paul's shoulders.

"About time," he grumbled. "You'd think I was dying or something with everyone hanging around like vultures ready to pick my bones clean."

"Come on, Tazer. Let's get that coffee we promised you hours ago before my inconsiderate brother decided to play the kamikaze musher."

Paul threw an empty pill cup at her. "Out!"

Kat grabbed Tazer's arm and ducked through the open door.

"See what I have to put up with? I practically kill myself and she thinks I did it on purpose." Paul shook his head, a grin teasing the corners of his lips.

Sam envied the camaraderie between brother and

sister. He let the good vibes chase away the bad as he steeled himself to tell Paul what really happened back on the trail.

By the time Emergency Medical Services arrived, Paul had regained consciousness and insisted he was fine. But because he'd been unconscious and there seemed to be damage to his ankle, they'd hauled him to the hospital. Kat rode alongside him in the back of the ambulance.

Sam stayed behind, insisting Vic and Tazer join Paul at the hospital. He'd taken the snowmobile and gone back out on the trail to retrieve his sled.

When he brought it back to the barn and gotten a good look at it, his heart ran as cold as the frozen river Paul had fallen on.

"What's wrong?" Paul asked, breaking into Sam's reverie. "Look, I must have been too close to the edge. It's not your fault I crashed."

"In a way it was."

Paul shook his head, a teasing look lifting the corners of his mouth. "I insisted on taking your sled. Apparently I wasn't ready for its superior speed and maneuverability."

"Paul, you don't understand." Sam held up a hand, stopping Paul's attempt to make him feel better about something that should never have happened. "That crash was no accident."

"What do you mean?" Paul punched the button adjusting the head of the bed upward.

"The stanchions had been cut clean through."

Silence followed as Paul's forehead wrinkled into a deep frown. "You sure they didn't break in the crash?"

"No, they were sawed at the base except a tiny piece to hold it temporarily." Sam's mouth tightened. "Someone did it deliberately. Someone who knew what to cut that wouldn't be obvious."

"Why?" Paul pressed his fingers to the bridge of his nose.

"I don't know, but that crash was intended for me, not you." Sam jammed his hands into his pockets and paced across the room and back.

"Assuming you're right and someone actually sabotaged your sled, it could just as easily have been mine. Yours sits next to mine in the barn."

"Correct, but everyone in Anchorage likes you." It was true. Sam hadn't met a soul in the city who had a bad word to say about Paul. "I'm the outsider stirring up trouble for the state."

"I bust people all the time. It could have been someone I put in jail," Paul argued.

"Yeah, but you don't have an entire political venue riding on your work." Or a past that might have caught up to him. Sam shrugged the thought away. No. He'd assumed a different identity when he'd left the agency. No one knew him by his new name or where he was except his old boss, Royce. As far as Sam was concerned, Russell Samson no longer existed. His old employer had helped him change all his records, even arranging for his name to be altered on his social-security card and Stanford University diploma to reflect his new identity.

"You're a geologist, not a politician, for Pete's

sake." Paul scooted into an upright sitting position, wincing as he moved.

"That ankle still hurt?" Sam asked.

"Yeah." The dark-haired man's lips twisted. "I'm waiting for the doctor to come back with the results of the X-rays."

"Think he'll bar you from the race?" Sam wished he hadn't let Paul borrow his sled. None of this would have happened—at least not to Paul.

Paul's forehead creased in a frown. "He'd better not. I've invested too much time and money to be excluded." Paul glanced up. "Any of your dogs injured?"

It was just like Paul to worry about the dogs more than himself. "No. They were fine. A little spooked, but once I untangled their necklines, they were raring to climb back up on the trail and run."

"Who would tamper with your sled?" Paul's brows furrowed. "Do you think it was another race contestant?"

"I can't imagine another musher considering me any kind of threat. I'm a complete rookie at mushing." Sam shook his head, the scent of alcohol and disinfectant starting to make his stomach churn. "However, I have so many people mad at me about the study, it could be anyone." His work in the interior had people up in arms on both sides of the political fence. On one side were those who wanted to open up more of the Alaskan interior to roads and progress. On the other side, the environmentalists were fighting tooth and nail to leave it relatively untouched.

"When do you head back to Washington?" Paul asked.

"After the race." A smile lifted his lips. "Senator Blalock is chomping at the bit to complete the study and get on with making a decision about oil production in the interior."

"Have you let on to anyone about the results?" Paul leaned forward. "You think the word leaked out?"

"I kept a pretty tight rein on the information. Blalock got a heads-up that the samples weren't good. Unless he let it slip to some bonehead in Washington, I don't know who else would know."

"It's too bad you can't let it out. At least the tree huggers would be off your back."

"Yeah, but Blalock is pretty rabid about finding oil out there. He was the one who got me hired on in the first place."

"It would be a big coup to bring in more oil to the country. I wouldn't think he'd be behind the sabotage, would he? Seems he'd be your best friend."

"Only if the results are what he wants to see." Sam pushed a hand through his hair. "Maybe I should pull out of the race altogether. The officials don't need more of a liability than they already have." And he didn't like not knowing who was after him.

"Are you kidding?" Paul's eyes widened. "You've worked as hard as anyone to prepare. No way. You're going."

"But if someone is after me, I'll only bring more trouble to everyone else in the race."

"Assuming someone is after you. Remember, my sled was next to yours. It could have been mine they meant to get. Especially since I plan to win the race this year." Paul leaned back and stared at the ceiling. "I wonder who would think they could only beat me by sabotaging my sled. We need to tell Kat. This is just the kind of puzzle she'd like."

"I'd rather not." Over the past two years, Sam had studied the pictures scattered around Paul's log cabin, pictures of Kat fishing, pictures of her with the dogs or behind a sled. Sam felt he knew more about her just from pictures than actually in person. She looked small but tough, feminine yet strong. A product of her upbringing.

Sam couldn't admit to Paul he'd harbored a secret attraction to Kat after hearing all the stories of their childhood in Alaska. Meeting her hadn't changed a thing. In fact, his respect grew even more because she didn't fall apart when Paul came in unconscious. Leanne would have called the ambulance and wrung her hands, carefully so as not to damage the expensive manicure.

No, Kat was down-to-earth and tough. From what Paul had told him, she had to be. She was in a dangerous business in some secret government organization. Paul had compared it to the CIA.

Sam suspected her job might be with the Stealth Operations Specialists, the business he'd been in while working in D.C. He could find out with a single phone call to Royce, but he refused to make contact with his old life.

Getting on with the S.O.S. wasn't easy. Kat had to have earned her position there for a reason and it wasn't based on her appearance. Although she'd left the room, Sam could still picture her jet-black hair as full and rich as Paul's and eyes as blue as glacier ice in the sunlight. If looks were all it took to get the job, she'd have gotten it hands down.

The woman foremost in his thoughts stepped through the door carrying two cups of coffee. She handed one to Sam and smiled. "Thought you could use a jolt." The smile transformed her otherwise serious face into a softer, more feminine version of her brother.

Sam got the feeling she hadn't smiled much over the past year. He remembered when Paul had flown out to D.C. to be with Kat at her husband's funeral a year ago. Had Marty been an agent, as well? Paul had come back saying Kat was okay, but Sam could tell Paul worried about his only sibling. And rightly so, judging by the dark circles beneath her eyes.

"Thanks." When he took the cup from her, their hands collided and an electric jolt speared through his system.

Kat's gaze shot up to his and just as quickly turned away. "Mind if I turn the television on?"

"Go ahead." Paul adjusted his pillow behind his head. "The local station is airing stories on each of the race contestants. Maybe we can size up the competition."

"You don't think you're racing still, do you?" Kat's brows rose and a hand fisted on her hip.

Paul's smile faded. He looked like a boy being told he can't go out to play. "My dogs are ready for this race. They deserve to participate."

"Maybe so, but we haven't even heard from the doctor. I don't think you can stand for twelve to fifteen days on that ankle."

Paul crossed his arms over his chest. "I'm not ruling it out until the doctor tells me different."

Sam would have smiled at the argument if he hadn't been so disturbed by his reaction to Kat's simple touch. He'd only just met the woman.

"They're kinda cute, aren't they?" Tazer leaned close to Sam, a grin playing across her model-perfect face.

She was gorgeous, but she reminded Sam too much of Leanne. He was immune to her kind of beauty. "Yes, she is," Sam responded. As soon as the words were out of his mouth, he realized his mistake.

Tazer's lips twitched, but that was the only acknowledgment of Sam's slip. "Kat's had a rough time of things." Her gaze swept to the woman arguing with her brother.

Sam took the opportunity to study Tazer while she wasn't looking in his direction. Did she work with Kat? Was she also an agent with the S.O.S.—assuming that was where Kat worked?

Though Sam wanted to ask all the questions spinning around in his mind, guilt nudged at his conscience. He didn't feel right talking about Kat with her standing only a few short steps away, but he couldn't help asking, "Is she still grieving for her husband?" He tried to tell himself he only cared out of mild curiosity.

"A little. I think his death shook her more than even she'll admit. Since then, she's been in a fog, like she doesn't know what she wants out of life. I'm glad she decided to come home." Tazer nodded toward Paul. "She needed her family."

Her family was still arguing with her. "My dogs will be in that race if I have to strap myself to the sled. I'm going."

Kat planted both fists on her hips, twin flags of red rising in her cheeks. "You couldn't drive the sled with a good foot, much less a broken one, otherwise you wouldn't be in the hospital now."

Sam's pulse quickened. This Kat was like a mama bear ready to take on the world to protect her cub. The determined stance and the heightened color made her even more beautiful than the pictures he'd stared at on the wall of her home.

"Tell her, Sam," Paul demanded.

He didn't want to be dragged into their domestic dispute. "Tell her what?"

"Tell her it wasn't my fault." Paul waved him forward. "Tell her why I crashed."

For some reason he couldn't fathom, he didn't want to get into the details of the accident. He resisted becoming another case to Kat. She was here on vacation, not to play investigative agent for a little prerace sabotage. Besides, Sam was fully qualified and capable of conducting his own investigation.

Kat's gaze pinned him, her eyes narrowing to slits. "Yes, please. Tell me why my brother crashed."

The direct look caught him off guard and he replied without hesitation. "The stanchions had been cut."

Her surprised gasp turned into an angry frown. "What did you say?"

In a flat tone, devoid of emotion, he explained, "The

struts holding the runners to the brushbow were cut at the base. It took a couple jolts and a sharp curve before they broke completely."

Paul crossed his arms over his chest and smiled. "I just happened to be on it at the time. So you see, it wasn't my fault."

Kat stared from Paul to Sam. "Who would do such a thing?"

Sam raised his hands. "I didn't. It was actually my sled that was cut. Paul was trying it out at the time."

"You're telling me this was deliberate?" The intensity of her gaze held his steady.

Sam nodded, his gut clenching at the memory of Paul lying unconscious at the bottom of the riverbank.

"Who would do such a thing?" she repeated with more righteous indignation, her blue eyes blazing.

"Looks like we're having a party in here," the doctor said from the open doorway. "Mind if I speak to the patient in private?"

"No, of course not," Kat said, yet she made no move to leave. As Sam passed her, she grabbed his arm. "We're not through talking about this."

That jolt struck him again. "Count on it." Sam stepped out into the hallway, shaking his arm as if he could shake free of the feeling of Kat's fingers touching him so easily.

"So, Sam, who's got it in for you?" Tazer joined him in the hospital corridor, closing the door behind her.

"Any number of people. I'm a geologist working oil exploration in the interior. People will either love what I'm doing, or hate it. No one straddles the fence."

Her eyes widened. "Oil and drilling are definitely hot topics with our current dependency on Middle Eastern sources."

"Between the environmentalists wanting me out and an Alaskan senator demanding that I give him the answer he wants, I'm pulled in two different directions."

"Either of which could have a motive to hurt you."

"Not to mention, the race on Saturday."

"Are there any competitors afraid you might win over them?" Tazer asked.

"I can't imagine someone thinking I was any kind of competition."

"You never know how the competitive mind works."

"Whatever. Paul shouldn't have been the one in the hospital. If I hadn't loaned my sled to him, he'd be fine."

She tapped a finger to her chin, her gaze running his length from head to toe. "And you would have been in the hospital or dead."

Sam inhaled a deep breath and let it out. "Yeah. Which leads back to the question of who."

"THE DOCTOR ONLY wanted to see me." Paul glared at Kat.

"As your only family, I need to hear what he has to say." Kat reached for his hand, refusing to take no for an answer.

The doctor's expression was too serious to be good news. He slipped an X-ray film into the lighted board on the wall and pointed at a bone close to the ankle. "You have a fracture in the medial malleolus." He turned to look at Paul, his face set in stern, no-nonsense lines. "You have a broken ankle."

"So?" Paul's face set in a stubborn frown. "Big deal. It's just the ankle."

"So—" the doctor glanced toward Kat briefly before leveling a hard stare at Paul "—you can't run the Iditarod on that fracture."

Paul's hand squeezed Kat's hard. "Are you sure? You're not mistaken? Look at it again." He pointed at the film.

"I'm certain. I recommend a cast and elevating your ankle for the next week to keep the swelling down. Six weeks in the cast ought to allow sufficient healing time."

"Six weeks?" Paul shouted. "I don't have two days to heal."

Kat patted his hand. "I think you missed the part where the doctor said you're not racing on Saturday."

"Since there is minimal swelling, I'll send the order up for the casting materials and have you fixed up in time to go home this afternoon." The doctor made notes on the chart and then looked up. "I'm sorry, Paul. But you need to take care of that bone and let it heal." On those parting words, the doctor left the room.

A long silence followed. Kat didn't know what to say to make it better. Paul trained hard all year long just to be in the Iditarod. To be so close to the race and not go was a fate almost worse than death to her brother. Kat knew. She'd been in several of the races and gone through the rigorous training with the dogs. She could feel Paul's disappointment like a palpable ache in her chest. "Look, Paul. There's always next year."

Paul's frown was fierce. "The dogs deserve to be in the race this year." He looked up into her face. "You know how much they love it."

"I know, and I know how much you love it. But you can't."

"Damn." For a long moment he stared at the wall. Then he grasped her hand, his face brightening. "I can't do it, but you can."

"No. Don't even think about it." She tried to pull her hand free. "What did that doctor give you for pain, anyway?"

"Only a little painkiller. I'm thinking straight, sis. You have to do it."

"No. I'm here to rest and relax. Not to spend two weeks in the freezing cold." Despite her protests, Kat felt a thrill of excitement flow through her veins. She hadn't felt that kind of kick since before Marty died. And it felt good. But still… "No. I haven't trained. The dogs won't be used to me. It's impossible."

"If you don't do it for me, do it for Sam. If someone is after him, he'll need protection. That's what you do, isn't it?"

Her heart stopped when she thought of Sam, the man she'd heard so much about from her brother in every e-mail, letter and phone call. The man who'd found his way into the family while she was out gallivanting around the world playing secret agent. Still, Sam cared about Paul, and Kat couldn't fault him for that.

But he made her nervous. With his sandy-blond hair,

gray-green eyes and a voice so smooth and penetrating it affected the functionality of her kneecaps. She wasn't sure she wanted to be anywhere near him. Marty had been dark and dangerous. Sam was everything Marty wasn't. He looked like the boy next door on steroids. His rugged outdoor tan and muscles would be enough to make her heart leap if she weren't still grieving for Marty. Okay, so the pain of Marty's death had faded quite a bit, but that didn't mean she was ready to jump back into the meat market of dating.

No. Being around Sam would not be good for her at this time. She'd been too vulnerable for too long. A place she hated being. Vulnerability wasn't something Jenkinses did well.

"You kinda like him, don't you?" Paul asked softly, grinning.

"No." But her no wasn't quite as definitive as before. She jerked her hand free of her brother's. "I have to get back and help Vic with the dogs. Call me when they have you all patched up and ready to come home."

"What?" He raised his hands. "You're not going to stay and hold my hand through the trauma of getting a cast? What kind of sister are you?"

She picked the paper cup off the floor where it had landed earlier and threw it at Paul's head. "Your worst nightmare."

"I knew that." His easy grin spread across his face. "But you're going to do the race."

The man was obviously high on some kind of pain-killer to think she'd jump into a race she hadn't trained for. She left the room in such a hurry, she bumped into Sam on his way in.

Her face flamed and she cursed herself, knowing how red she could get. She ducked her head and turned her back on Sam. "Tazer, you ready to go back to the house?"

"Whenever you are," she said, her posture as relaxed as it was poised to handle anything.

"Oh, I'm ready, all right." Ready to get away from her brother and the man who'd gone into the room after she left. So what if he might be in trouble and needed her kind of protection. "What part of *off duty* doesn't he understand?" she muttered.

"Are you expecting an answer?" Tazer glanced down at her perfect nails. "Because if you are, the answer is an S.O.S. agent is never off duty."

Trust Tazer to put it all in perspective. Kat rolled her eyes. "Thanks." She layered a boatload of sarcasm into the one word.

"You're welcome." Tazer stared across the shiny tiled floor at Kat. "I haven't seen you this animated in a long time."

"Comes from being surrounded by crazy Alaskans and an insane brother."

"He's kinda cute, isn't he?"

Tazer's sly smile sent warning signals through Kat. "He's my brother."

"Yeah, him, too, but I was thinking more of Sam." Her gaze pinned Kat's.

The woman was fishing. But she wasn't going to

catch anything in this pond. "If you like the boy-next-door look. Me, I prefer a man with more mystery."

"So, does that mean you're finally thinking about other men?"

The spunk went out of her spine and Kat sagged against the wall. "No. I'm not thinking about dating other men." Although Sam sprang to mind, uninvited.

"I didn't say date. I said 'thinking about.'" Tazer's lips twitched.

Kat sighed. "Think…date…whatever."

"Look, Kat, you're intelligent, pretty and too young to give up on love. Don't let Marty's death take you out of the running completely."

"Says the woman who swore off men even before she graduated high school." As soon as the words left her lips, Kat regretted them.

Tazer straightened, her lips firming into a tight line. "I have good reasons."

"I know." Kat pushed off the wall and laid a hand on Tazer's arm. "I'm sorry. I shouldn't have said that."

Tazer had been raped when she was only sixteen years old. Not many people knew that. Tazer had sworn from that point on, she'd never be in a position where a man overpowered her again, and she'd lived up to her own promise.

Kat squeezed her arm. "You deserve to find love more than I do. I had it once."

"This isn't about me." Tazer shrugged off Kat's hand. "It's about you. Don't think you can sidetrack me into discussing my love life."

Kat snorted. "Or lack thereof."

"You took the plunge once. It was good, but *he* died."

Kat winced. "Could you soften it up just a little?"

"No. You need the cold hard truth. Just because Marty died doesn't mean you have to die with him. He was full of life and excitement. He'd want you to go on."

The back of Kat's throat closed and she fought for control. "I know. Just don't push me. I'm not ready."

Tazer's gaze softened. "Fair enough. I've been known to be pushy on occasion."

Kat barked a shaky laugh. "Try all the time."

"I wouldn't be such a pushy bitch if I didn't care."

"I know." Kat smiled. She couldn't ask for a truer friend.

Tazer was known for her straightforward, call-it-like-it-is lack of sugarcoating. But she was there when Kat needed her. "What's the doctor's verdict on your brother?"

"He'll live, but he can't race on Saturday or anytime in the next six weeks."

Tazer frowned. "I guess that means you'll be taking up the reins or whatever it is you call the steering wheel on a dogsled, huh?"

"Handlebar," Kat answered automatically before she thought through what Tazer said. She threw her hands in the air. "What's with you and Paul thinking I'm ready to jump into the race from hell after barely arriving in the state?"

"Look, sweetie, you can deny it all you want, but you know you love it. That's all you used to talk about when you first came to the agency."

"Was I that bad?"

"Worse." Her smile softened her words. "I learned more than I ever wanted to know about dogs, sleds and mushing. If you don't do this race, I'll kick your butt from here all the way back to D.C. Besides, it's your duty to be there in case tall, blond and gorgeous gets into trouble."

"If I do this race—and I'm not saying I will—it'll be because of the sabotage, not because I want to race."

"You say potato, I say potahto. As long as you get the job done. I'll let the boss know you're on the clock."

"Great, one more person to twist my arm on this."

"You don't need to race." That deep voice that made her knees act funny spoke from the doorway behind her. "You haven't been training. It wouldn't be advisable."

Kat spun to face Sam, her heart hammering faster than was warranted. "You don't think I can make it?" Wobbly knees stiffened and her jaw firmed.

"Paul should know better than to throw you into a race you're not ready for."

Her hackles rose but she kept her face pokerstraight. "Don't you think I'm capable of making my own decisions?" She planted a sweet smile on her face, ignoring the scent of his aftershave, a tantalizing aroma she tried to tell herself she didn't even like. But she'd be lying.

He stood with his feet slightly spread and his arms crossed over his chest. "It's your funeral."

Who did this Norse god think he was, telling her she couldn't hack a little eleven-hundred-mile race? Forcing confidence she really didn't feel, she smiled up at him.

"Thanks." Then she turned to her brother, her blood slamming through her veins. "If it's all the same to you, bro, I'll be taking your dogs on the Iditarod."

Chapter Three

If Sam thought it would have done any good, he'd have argued until he was blue. But from what he'd learned from Paul, Kat was a stubborn woman. When she settled on an idea, she held on to it like a pit bull in a dogfight. If he hadn't been worried about her, he might have appreciated her confidence and strong will.

Luck of the draw had Sam leaving as number twenty-seven at the Wasilla start point behind Paul's twenty-three. Or should he say Kat's twenty-three? The officials had approved the replacement at the last minute, knowing her past racing history.

Sam had barely spoken to Paul and Kat the past two days. He felt as if Paul had coerced her into following Sam to keep him safe. He didn't like the idea of being assigned a babysitter to dog his every step on the trail. He didn't need anybody to watch his back.

He packed his rifle and handgun in the three hundred pounds of gear and equipment on the sled. Many mushers brought weapons in the event a cranky moose decided to attack. If animal or human tried something funny during the race, Sam was prepared.

Paul insisted Kat was only taking over his position in the competition because his dogs deserved a chance to win. Sam knew better. Paul was more worried about the sabotage than his dogs making a good show.

As the dogs dipped down into a ravine and back up to climb the slight rise before Knik, Sam braced himself for the onslaught. Well-wishers lined the path to see family and friends off at the last stop before they headed into the wilderness.

A slew of people milled about at the checkpoint with a collection of trucks scattered across the snow.

"Whoa!" Sam called out to his team. He eased down on the brake, digging the snow hook into the hard-packed snow as he pulled to a stop next to Vic's old pickup.

Paul sat inside, with the door open, his injured foot wrapped in a blanket and secured with duct tape.

With her coat collar pulled up around her cheeks, Tazer stood beside the truck, a soft gray headband protecting her ears from the bitter wind, her nose bright pink.

Working with the veterinarian, Vic walked the line of dogs, scanning microchips, checking paws, booties and necklines until they reached the sled.

"You're good to go." The vet checked off the paperwork and nodded before heading off to the next arrival.

Sam flexed his gloved hands, tugged his wool scarf down below his chin and strode over to the truck.

"Kat pulled through ten minutes ago." Paul reached out a hand and shook Sam's. "She said she'd meet you at Yentna, if you can catch her. All I can say is good luck, buddy. She's a tough competitor. And my team knows her and vice versa."

Sam nodded, relieved Kat planned to compete rather than play nursemaid to him. Although he'd kept his eyes open for signs of her powder-blue jacket and pants.

A large white van armed with satellite dishes, antennas and the bright red logo of the local Anchorage television station stood to one side. A cameraman and female reporter watched for the next contestant.

A sled pulled in behind Sam and, as if on cue, the reporter pushed the hair out of her face and the scarf away from her mouth before turning to the cameraman.

"What's all that about?" Sam asked.

"Looks like Al Fendley's team." Vic shook his head. "Never fails, he manages to get the best press for the race."

Paul studied the man in the showy yellow parka, smiling broadly and stepping from the runners of his sled like a movie actor on set. "'Course, it doesn't hurt to get free publicity for your business."

The name sounded familiar, but Sam couldn't place it. "What does he do?"

"He and his brother, Warren, run a summer lodge and dogsled training camp outside of Denali Park. They also have a hunting-outfitter business in the interior." Vic brushed the snow off his gloves. "Al got a name for himself when he won the race two years ago."

Paul glanced across at Al. "I hear one of the other mushers fell out of the race when his dogs got sick that year."

"Tough break," Sam said. "It's a long race. I can imagine the dogs take a beating over the eleven hundred miles."

"Not when you're neck in neck, only a day out from the finish line and your brother is one of the folks helping with the food drops." Vic's gaze collided with Paul's. "Rumor had it the dogs were slipped a mild poison at one of the checkpoints. The Fendley boys take winning seriously."

After a narrow-eyed glance at Al, Paul turned his attention to Sam. "Take care out there. You're a long way from civilization if anything happens."

Sam knew the dangers of the Iditarod. "I'd better get going."

"Oh, before you go." Tazer stepped up to Sam. "Kat wanted me to give you something."

His hand went out automatically and jerked back when she tried to place a radio and headset into his gloved palm. "What the hell is it?"

"A two-way radio and voice-activated mic. You two can keep in touch in case you have trouble on the trail."

"No way." He recognized the standard-issue radio from his days working for the S.O.S. He'd given up that life long ago and he didn't intend to go back. Still, he shouldn't have reacted so strongly. Sam's lips pressed into a tight line. "I'm not interested."

"In the radio or Kat?"

He glared at the woman. "Either."

"Please, Sam," Paul said from his position on the seat of the truck. "I usually go along on the race when Kat's out there. I'd feel better knowing she had you looking out for her."

"If this is your way of putting Kat on me for protection, no deal." Sam shook his head. "I can take care of myself."

"I know you can take care of yourself," Paul said. "What I'm worried about is that it could have been either me or you they were after. If it's someone wanting to win the race at all costs, any one of the teams and mushers could be in trouble. I'd feel better knowing you were looking after my little sister."

The little-sister part hit Sam square in the gut. If he'd said Kat, the government agent, Sam might have told him which cliff to jump off. But Kat, the little sister, was another story altogether. Sam had a little sister back in Virginia. A grown-up little sister with a life of her own working as a legislative assistant to a congressman. If someone posed a threat to his only family left, he'd be equally concerned. "You play dirty, Jenkins."

Without batting an eyelash, Paul grinned. "Damn right I do. Got to take care of my two favorite mushers."

"Kat can take care of herself," Sam noted. "Or so she says."

"Oh, she can," Paul agreed. "But it never hurts to have backup."

Tazer held the radio out. "Does that mean you'll wear it?"

With a sigh, Sam took the equipment and adjusted the headset to fit in his ear, tucking the radio into his pocket.

Tazer reached out and flipped the On switch. "Say something."

"I don't have time to talk. I have to get back in the race," Sam grumbled.

"That you, Sam?" Kat's voice sounded soft and smooth.

Blood flowed through his system like warm molasses and he fought the spreading heat. "Why didn't you pin this thing on me yourself?" Then again, that might not have been a good idea. For the past few days, they'd worked side by side to complete preparations for the race, bagging feed for the drops, packing and repacking their sleds and tending to the dogs. He'd bumped into her more than he cared for.

Kat chuckled. "Tazer has a way with pinning unlike any other."

Tazer's brows rose. "Tell Kat to keep her eye on the trail and a hand on her gun, just to be safe." Then she turned toward Paul. "Got room for me up there? It's getting damn cold out here."

Paul scooted over, easing his ankle out of the door frame.

Tazer climbed into the truck next to Paul and smiled. "Don't break her heart, will ya?"

Sam frowned. "Who?"

Paul chuckled from the interior of the truck. "Buddy, you've been out in the woods too long." His smile faded. "Take care out there."

Other teams were arriving, heralded by the barking of sixty dogs.

"The team's all set." Vic clapped a hand to Sam's back. "Better get going if you want to make use of the remaining daylight."

Sam pulled the scarf up over his mouth and nodded to Paul, Vic and Tazer before he stepped on the sled, pulled up the snow hook and yelled, "Let's go!"

KAT HAD A HARD TIME slowing the team. They were trained to race, to go for as long and as hard as they could before they needed rest. Stopping every hour to waste fifteen minutes made the lead dogs nervous and the rest of the team impatient. Already, several teams passed her. Her team howled in protest when she applied the brake and snow hook.

As much as Paul wanted her to win this race, she couldn't go off without Sam. He was the only reason she'd agreed to the race in the first place.

Now that she was out on the snow, a world away from the hustle and crowds of D.C., she was glad she'd agreed. She couldn't ask for a better place to think, unimpeded by the well-meaning S.O.S. team or her family back at the house. Royce had told her to get away from it all. Hell, he'd practically kicked her out of the office, insisting she needed the downtime. Nothing like being on the last frontier to get away from it all.

With the cold wind in her face, making ice crystals form in her eyelashes, and the soft sound of the runners skimming across the crusty snow, she relaxed.

"Is this thing still working?"

Sam's clear crisp voice in Kat's ear jolted her back to reality. A muffled tapping sound beat against her eardrum.

Kat winced. "I can hear you. Can you hear me?"

"Yes."

"Then it works." She could picture him frowning, and fiddling with the equipment, his gloved hands too bulky to be of much use with the small radio-transmitting device.

"Where'd they put the damn Off switch?" he asked.

"There's a tiny switch on the piece that fits in the ear, but since we've got these things, we might as well use them."

"Feels funny having a woman in my head."

Kat chuckled. "No funnier than having a man in mine."

"Just to set the record straight, I don't need your protection for this race. If anything, I'm out here as your protection."

"Sure, whatever you say." Most men resisted having a woman provide protection of any kind—as if they conceded to being less of a man if they had a woman running interference.

"We don't know that the accident was anything more than a onetime deal," Sam continued.

"No, we don't," she answered smoothly, but Kat knew better. After inspecting the sled herself, she knew the damage had been deliberate. Question was, whose sled had the saboteur intended?

Sam sighed softly in her ear. "I don't know about you, but I'm out here to win this race."

Kat smiled behind the heavy wool neck scarf. "Sure you are. Like all the other sixty-six entrants and me."

"That's right." He paused. "So look out, it won't be long before you're eating my dust."

"Snow." Kat couldn't help correcting him. He needed it. The man was too independent. A lot like Marty. Determined to make it on his own and damn anyone who got in the way. That was one of the characteristics Kat had loved about Marty.

"Snow?"

"Eating my snow. We hope there's not much dust at this time of year."

Sam laughed in her ear, the sound warming Kat from the inside out. "Are you always this disagreeable?"

"Only when I'm confronted by a disagreeable man."

"Point taken," he conceded.

"I thought you didn't like talking into these things."

"I don't."

"Then shut up and get moving."

His gentle snort was the last sound he made for a while.

When Kat realized she was still grinning, her lips turned downward. Where had that lighthearted feeling come from? And had she just been flirting with the man?

Sam was all right. For a transplant from Virginia, he seemed to understand the nature, care and feeding of the animals. And the dogs liked him.

Even Loki treated him like a member of the pack and Loki was a better judge of human character than most people. If Loki liked you, most likely, you were a good person. Not that Kat formed her impressions of strangers on the recommendation of a dog. Sam might have proven himself in the kennels, but would he have the stamina and drive to complete the eleven-hundred-mile race?

No matter whether he did or not, Kat planned to. Not so much to win as to prove to herself she still had it in her. She might have left Alaska for a few years, but the blood running through her veins was still ninety percent melted tundra snow.

Over the next hour of silence, the only sounds coming over the radio were the occasional commands Sam gave his team.

As she neared a good resting point, Kat asked, "Where are you?"

"Passed the Nome sign a few miles back."

The famous Nome sign indicated only another one thousand forty-nine miles to go to the finish line. Kat's breath always caught in her throat when her sled moved past the sign. Knowing she had so many more miles to go could be overwhelming, but not insurmountable. "You should be nearing Fish Creek. Watch out for the fifty-foot drop into the ravine. I almost spilled there. How are you holding up?" She didn't know Sam or his abilities as a musher. He appeared to be in good condition and probably was from all the tromping around retrieving soil and mineral samples or whatever he did as a geologist.

"Don't worry about me. I'm the one who's been training for this event."

She chuckled. "Think I'm not up to it?"

He paused before answering. "If the snowshoe fits…"

"I have to admit, the cold is a little more than I'm

used to, but I'll be fine after a couple days." Physically, she'd never been in better shape. After Marty's death, she'd poured herself into exercise and fitness. If not for any other reason than to eat up time between missions.

Lonely, empty time.

When friends, like Tazer, tried to include her in outings, trips or movies, she'd declined, retreating into her own world, preferring to handle her loss alone.

Kat removed one gloved hand from the handlebar and flexed her fingers. She'd been on the trail for four hours, the dogs were still full of energy and running, but they needed regular rest stops and snacks to keep up the pace.

Crisscrossed by snowmobile tracks, the trail opened onto a wide frozen swamp packed down by hundreds more snowmobile tracks. With trees bordering the swamp, this was where she usually made her first stop to rest the dogs. The copse of trees ahead and to the right would provide a good windbreak for her and the huskies. If Sam was making good time, he should catch up soon. She could get her cooker going and snack the dogs in that time.

"Gee!" Kat shouted the command, her voice carrying easily through the silence to her lead dogs.

Loki and Eli pulled to the right, the rest of the team falling in line.

As the dogs entered the stand of trees, Kat eased onto the foot brake and set out the snow hook, slowing the animals to a stop. Loki and Eli flopped to the ground, alert but relaxed with their heads on their paws. Some of the younger dogs danced around on their necklines before settling in for a rest.

After checking the feet, booties and general condition of the line of dogs, Kat fired up the portable cooker. Before long she had snow melting for the dog food and water boiling for coffee.

The dogs heard the arrival of another team before Kat could see them. They appeared from around a curve in the trail, tiny, dark dots in the white of the snow, growing larger as they neared.

The dogs slid in beside hers and stopped with a lot of tail wagging, happy yips of greeting and sniffing.

Kat handed Sam a canteen cup of coffee and turned to his sled and dogs. "Any problems?"

With Sam on one side and Kat on the other side of the team, they walked the line of dogs, checking feet, wrists and shoulders. All appeared in good shape.

After the dogs were fed and taken care of, Sam gave Kat a narrow-eyed look. "Look, if you're slowing up for me, forget it. I'm here to race. I'll leave you so far behind you won't catch up." His gray-green eyes flashed in the late-afternoon sun.

She tipped her head to the side. "Is that a challenge?"

"You bet."

"You're on." She tossed the remains of her canteen cup into the snow, and stowed the metal cooker and feeding dishes before climbing on the back of her sled.

The sound of a snowmobile alerted her that they were no longer alone. The trail was not exclusive to the sled teams. Occasional snowmobiles were encountered, especially early on in the race when they hadn't completely left civilization behind. Kat only gave it minor consideration. She pulled up the snow hook and had sucked in a lungful of air to shout to her team, when a shot rang out.

Sam's cap flew from his head. "What the hell?"

Kat's team yelped and lunged forward. She barely caught the handlebar with her gloved fingertips, struggling for a few seconds to hang on. She stepped on the foot brake to slow the dogs. When she turned back toward Sam, he lay on the ground.

"Get down!" he yelled. "Someone just shot at me."

"Whoa!" Kat dropped to a crouch, anchoring her snow hook to keep the dogs from leaving with the sled. "Are you okay?" She scanned the tree line across the swamp.

"I'm fine." As he reached out to grab his hat, another shot echoed through the stillness and his hat leaped into the air. "What the h—"

"Stay down." Kat dropped to her stomach. "I'll move around the clearing to see if I can find out who's shooting."

"You'll stay exactly where you are," Sam hissed into the mic. "I'll go check."

"Look, I'm trained in this kind of maneuver."

"So am I," he gritted out. "Stay down."

"If I were a man, would you be so concerned?"

"Now is not the time to go all equal opportunity on me."

Kat scooted behind the bulk of her fully laden sled. "Chauvinist." Although frustrated by his demand for her to stay, she didn't say the word in anger. With a man shooting at him, she didn't wish additional bad karma on Sam.

"I won't have another man, woman…or child…die on my account," Sam muttered, working his way around to the opposite side of his sled. He dug into the pouch containing his rifle. With the weapon in front of him, he ran in a zigzag pattern toward the trees.

Shots rang out, hitting the snow just in front of or behind his boots.

Kat's breath caught in her throat. Sam certainly looked as if he knew what he was doing. She hoped like hell he did.

Chapter Four

With bullets hitting too damn close for comfort, Sam dropped behind a fallen log, easing around the side to scan the area. Another shot echoed across the clearing. Dirt and splinters from the log sprayed his cheek. In a low crawl, he scrambled the length of the fallen trunk until he reached a stand of trees with a clump of bushes at its foot. Based on the direction his hat flew off, the bullets came out of the north. Besides his own breathing and that of Kat's stirring against her microphone, Sam didn't hear anything. All thirty-two dogs sensed the danger and waited, ears perked, alert and silently awaiting orders.

Sam straightened and stood behind the relative safety of a tree. "Let's see how good a shot he is," he muttered.

"Oh, please tell me you're not going to give him a target," Kat growled into the mic. "Just what I need, a man with a death wish."

Okay, so maybe the mic was sensitive enough to pick up muttering. "Don't think you're getting off so easily. I'm going to make it to the finish line."

Was that a feminine snort? "Intact, I hope." Kat Sikes was a livewire and not afraid to speak her mind.

Sam grinned and slid his glove halfway off his hand, then poked it around the side of the tree.

A bullet smacked into it and flung the glove five feet behind him, confirming his suspicion, but leaving one hand gloveless and cold. "This guy's a professional sniper."

"I feel better knowing that." Kat's voice dripped sarcasm.

"The good news is he's after me."

Kat laughed, the sound blasting into Sam's ear. "You think that's good news?"

"Better than him being after everyone in the race, including you. I'm going to circle the clearing." He glanced around, spotting another fair-size tree ten yards away. "This guy can't get away."

"Don't do it, Sam."

"What would you suggest? Stand here until he decides he's played long enough?" Although she couldn't see him, he shook his head, the bite of cold air already numbing his exposed fingers. "You know how to use a gun?"

"Don't make me laugh." An audible click sounded in his ear, a clear indication she was armed and ready. "Gotcha covered."

"Don't shoot unless you have to. No use giving him his next target."

"I'll be the judge of that." She was cocky and fearless. The combination could be admirable or foolhardy. Sam hoped it didn't make a lethal combination. He pushed away from the tree and ran for the next, his path erratic and as unpredictable as he could make it. Weighed down by heavy, insulated boots and snow, he moved slower than he liked. If he was lucky, the sniper wouldn't draw a decent bead on him.

A bullet snapped a branch beside his cheek, another tore through his bulky parka, missing his arm by a hair.

"Son of a—" Kat swore. "I can't see the bastard." She fired a couple rounds.

"Aim for that outcropping of trees on the far side of the swamp." Sam pushed away from the safety of the trees and ran again. At this rate, he'd be on the other guy by tomorrow. This time, he ran longer and faster through skeletal underbrush laced with snow.

The rain of bullets ceased when he'd gone only halfway, leading Sam to believe his attacker hadn't stuck around. He continued until he'd circled the clearing.

Meanwhile, Kat had gone quiet, as well.

Sam missed the steady stream of sarcasm he'd gotten used to. "You still with me?"

"I'm with you," she responded in a breathless voice.

Sam didn't have time to ponder the reason she was winded all of a sudden. In the distance a small engine roared to life.

"Sounds like our friend flew the coop," Kat commented.

"Damn." Sam arrived at the outcropping of trees with the absolute certainty he wouldn't find his man.

The snow was packed down and bullet casings littered the ground.

Sam lifted one spent shell from the snow and dropped it in his pocket. Then he followed the footsteps up and over a small rise. This swamp area was known for the multitude of snowmobile tracks crisscrossing through the area. Another set of snowmobile tracks wasn't unusual. Except the driver had been shooting at Sam. He couldn't chalk the incident up to a hunter mistaking him for a moose.

A branch snapped behind him and Sam spun.

"Whoa, tiger." Kat held up her hands, her rifle in one of them. "I'm on your side." She stared out at the packed snow. "You'll never trace him. There are too many tracks around here to even try."

"I know." He glanced at her, a frown drawing his brows downward. "I thought I told you to stay put."

"In case you haven't figured it out yet, I don't always follow orders." She shrugged. "It's a hard habit to break. Ask my brother."

"The sniper could just as easily shoot you as me."

She tipped her head to the side, her brows rising on her forehead. "But he wasn't aiming for me, was he?"

"No, he was after me." Sam shook his head. "I'd sure as hell like to know why."

"We can report the incident at our next checkpoint. But if we don't get on the trail, we won't make it before midnight."

"I'd rather not report the shooting. If he's only after me, why shut down an entire race?"

"Are you nuts or do you really have a death wish?"

Sam ignored her and retraced his footsteps to retrieve

his glove. Fortunately, only one finger had a hole in the tip. Nothing a little duct tape wouldn't cure.

Kat followed, grumbling the entire way.

Her anger only managed to make Sam smile. He liked to get under her skin and make her blue eyes flash. The race was definitely going to be interesting for more than one reason.

Once they checked the dogs, they both stepped behind the runners of their sleds and raised their snow hooks.

"Let's go!" Sam and Kat shouted simultaneously.

Anxious to leave the frozen swamp behind, both teams strained against their harnesses. Kat and Sam barely had time to grab their handlebars before the sleds jerked forward.

Despite the near miss, they still had a race to complete with approximately a thousand miles left to go.

Sam let Kat take the lead. During the next four hours, he debated turning back. A maniac wanted him dead or at least scared. No, if he'd wanted him dead, why would someone want to shoot at him and miss?

KAT LIFTED ONE HAND from the handlebar and readjusted her scarf over her face, covering the exposed skin up to the edge of her goggles. The temperature had dropped in the past four hours since the sun sank below the horizon. At the Yentna checkpoint it had been minus six. It must be nearing minus twenty now. The sky was clear, the stars shining bright on the trail and not a single fluffy cloud hovered over this lonely part of Alaska to help keep the relative heat of the day from escaping into the atmosphere.

The Alaskan huskies loved the cold; their mix of breeds, including greyhound, husky and other dogs, combined speed with strength and endurance. Their bodies were equipped to handle extreme temperatures. They ran as if they would never get tired, but Kat knew better. After she collected her food bags and straw from the Skwentna checkpoint, she planned to rest them for several hours.

Lights from a small cluster of buildings loomed ahead, as well as the lights from dozens of snowmobiles lining the trail. A cheer went up and continued, as well-wishers shouted encouragement to Kat, then Sam following half a mile behind.

Kat loved the Iditarod, the sense of everyone being in it together, the support of the locals and volunteers along the way and the beauty of Alaska. Her heart swelled with pride that she was one of them. One of the lucky people born and raised in this great state.

As she slid into the Skwentna checkpoint, she pressed her foot to the brake. "Whoa." The dogs barked excitedly to the other twenty teams already there. The noise was unrelenting and exhilarating all at once. The team didn't act as though they'd been on the trail for over nine hours. They were ready to visit and play with members of their own kind.

Sam joined her. "Stopping here?"

"No. Too busy around here for the dogs to get any real rest. I thought we'd stop a few miles out to get a jump on tomorrow's time."

"Sure you don't want the safety of numbers?"

"Believe me, there will be numbers we can mix with in the smaller camp farther down the trail." A racing official directed them to their feed bags. Once she'd lugged the bag to her sled and tied it down, she headed for a stack of straw and grabbed a bale.

"Need help with that?" Sam dug his hands into a bale and hefted it with little effort.

Grumpy and starting to feel the strain of stress and fatigue, Kat shot him a glare. "No, thank you. I can pull my own weight in the race."

Sam had the nerve to chuckle. "Not as in shape as you thought?"

Her glare deepened, but she didn't refute his words. Truth was that jogging and lifting weights was only half the effort needed to be physically prepared to lead a team on the grueling race. Her shoulders ached and her hands cramped with the effort of hanging on to the sled over the rolling terrain.

Sam tossed his bale on top of his sled and tied it down. Kat admired how easily he accomplished the task, gloved hands and all.

Meanwhile, she struggled to lift hers to the top of the loaded sled. Once she had her bale in place, she walked the line of dogs, snacking them once more.

Back at the sled, she stripped off a glove and dug in one of her pockets, retrieving her satellite phone, an illegal addition to her equipment by Iditarod standards. Given the circumstances, Kat deemed it necessary. She walked around to the back of a building out of sight and sound of the other contestants. After the shooting in the swamp, she'd called Tazer to fill her in. Now she was anxious for a status update.

From where she stood, she could just see Sam bent over his lead dogs' feet.

Tazer answered on the first ring. "Hey, Kat. How's everything going? You make the checkpoint at Skwentna yet?"

"We're there now." She glanced at Sam, putting fresh booties on Striker's and Hammer's feet. Even covered from head to foot in thick layers of clothing, he exuded strength and a sincere concern for his team.

"Anything on who might have been shooting at us? Anything on Sam's work that could make someone angry enough to want to kill him?"

"As a matter of fact, I just got information on one of the race contestants." Papers rustled and Tazer continued, "Al Fendley is a hunting outfitter. It's no secret he wants Sam to find oil in the interior to open up more roads north in the area of his hunting operation."

"Is that enough for him to want to have Sam killed?" Kat stared across at Sam.

"Apparently Al's up to his eyeteeth in debt from expanding his outfitter business. He even flew in building supplies to have a lodge constructed in the proposed drilling area."

"Jumped the gun, did he?"

"Yeah." Tazer hesitated then added, "There's something else."

Sam straightened, scanning the crowd in front of

the building. His search continued until he spotted her and he smiled.

Kat's pulse quickened. "What else?"

"When I called Royce to discuss the situation with Sam, he only sounded mildly concerned. When I called in the update about the shooting, he sounded funny."

"Funny? What did he say?"

"He said, 'Sam can handle it.'"

"What?" Kat frowned, her gaze on Sam.

His eyes narrowed and he headed across the snow toward her.

Not wanting Sam to overhear her conversation or read her lips, Kat turned her back to him. "Why would he say that? Does he know Sam?"

"I didn't think so, but now I'm not so sure." Tazer's voice lowered. "When I asked if you two should drop out of the race, Royce was adamant you stay in. He said, and I repeat verbatim, 'Kat and Sam are good. If the shooter isn't just after Sam, they need to be there for the rest of the participants.'"

An image of Sam moving through the trees around the swamp came to Kat's mind. He'd used all the cover, concealment and movement techniques of a combat veteran. "How would he know if Sam was good or not?"

"How would who know what about me?" Sam asked over Kat's shoulder.

"Look, Tazer, I gotta get back on the trail. Will you follow up and let me know what you find out?"

"Sure. Keep your head down, girl."

"Will do." She ended the call and tucked the satellite

phone in her pocket before she turned to face Sam. Questions burned a hole in her tongue. S.O.S. was supposed to stay secret. If she asked Sam how Royce Fontaine knew him, she'd open up herself to a barrage of questions from Sam. If she did that, she might risk losing her cover. Kat chewed on her bottom lip. Damn.

"Why didn't you tell me you had a satellite phone?" Kat shot a look around, afraid someone might have seen her using the device. "Actually, they're against the rules."

Sam's brows rose and a half smile lifted one side of his mouth. "Kat Sikes breaking a rule?"

She shrugged, slipping her glove over her fingers. "I weighed the risks and, given the circumstances, felt the phone was a rule worth sacrificing." She stepped up to her sled, slid goggles over her eyes and tugged her scarf up to cover her face, a good shield to hide her expression. "Ready to go? I don't know about you, but I could eat a caribou and I'm sure the dogs are ready for a rest."

Sam frowned, his lips pressing together.

"See ya in a few." Kat didn't wait for his response. She snagged a volunteer, who led her through the maze of contestants and dogs, past the Idita-trash and piles of loose straw. Another team sailed by her, the dogs brushing close to hers, going too fast for the tight quarters of the checkpoint. A camera crew turned floodlights on the driver, blinding Kat in the process. Anger burned through her at the musher's rudeness.

The bright yellow parka was none other than Al Fendley. The man played to the camera at the expense, not only of his safety, but the safety of the animals and other contestants. Never mind his dogs could easily have gotten tangled in her dogs' necklines, injuring both teams in the process.

Al didn't slow for a moment, barreling through until he cleared the crowd, the dogs running all out, making a good show for the camera. The man was rude and lacking any concern for his fellow racers, but did that make him a killer?

The volunteer leading Loki shook his head and continued moving steadily through the throng until the path cleared and all that stood between her team and the trail was crisp night air. Kat took a deep, calming breath and shouted, "Let's go!"

The dogs shot forward with Kat hanging tightly to the handlebar. "Thanks," she called over her shoulder to the volunteer.

A quick glance to her rear revealed another volunteer leading Sam's team to the edge of the crowd. With quiet determination, Sam pulled his clothing into place before he grabbed the handlebar and shouted, "Let's go!"

As she left the lights of Skwentna behind, darkness enveloped her. Once her eyes adjusted to the moonlight, Kat switched the headlamp off. She could clearly see the dark silhouette of Loki far ahead. Without the lamp, she was less of a target to a shooter. Sam's team fell in behind her, lights out and keeping pace. Nothing but the night and the sound of the runners scraping along the icy, packed snow pierced the silence. She could almost forget she'd had another life before coming home. Almost. Images of Royce Fontaine coming to her apartment in the middle of the night flashed through her memories, blinding her to the beauty of the stars. The night he'd come to tell her Marty died.

Her chest clenched and the sled hit a hard patch of crusty snow churned up by the hundreds of snowmobiles that had traveled these trails a few weeks earlier in the annual Iron Dog race. The jolt forced her to concentrate on the rough surface, on the team in front of her and the hazards ahead.

With someone shooting at Sam, she didn't have the time or luxury to ruminate about the past. Kat couldn't let her guard down for a minute. Thoughts of Marty would have to wait until she'd completed the Iditarod and went back to Washington. Whoever had been shooting at them earlier might be looking for another opportunity to do it again.

The question was how far would he follow them to make good his commitment to kill Sam? The man was clearly a professional. Traversing a clearly marked trail, they would be exposed more times that she could count. Would Kat be able to stop him?

A chill that had nothing to do with the frigid temperature slithered down her back and suddenly the shadows cast by the moonlight filled with sinister monsters waiting to pounce.

A DULL ACHE had settled at the base of Sam's skull. This early in the race, the trail was rutted and packed by the many snowmobiles that used these paths to travel between isolated villages. The constant jolting and balancing on the runners of the sled for the past nine hours had taken their toll. A four-hour rest would be nice about now. Sam hoped Kat felt the same. Two hours just didn't give them enough time to feed the dogs, much less catch a few hours of sleep themselves.

If they didn't get rest while there were plenty of people around, he couldn't see getting rest farther along in the race. Long gaps would stretch between the participants, leaving them out in the open, exposed to a persistent sniper.

Sam wondered how far his pursuer would go into the race before he grew tired of the cold. Another day? Two? A week? Would he follow him deep into the mountains where he could dispose of the body with a slim chance of finding it until the spring melts, if at all?

The sled lurched to the side and Sam leaned the other way to compensate. His gut told him the man was still out there, watching. Maybe laying in wait to try again.

But if he was such a good shot, why had he purposely missed earlier that day?

The answer was obvious. He hadn't wanted to kill Sam then. Like a cat playing with a mouse, he wanted to toy with his prey for a while before he killed him.

Sam hoped the brave woman in front of him didn't get caught in the crossfire.

The trail climbed into the Shell Hills, narrowing, twisting and turning through the woods. Trees stood close together, their dark trunks like silent sentinels.

Sam let the distance lengthen between his team and Kat's to avoid running over her if she slowed to take a curve. She'd long since moved out of sight and he wasn't sure he liked that.

"Talk to me, Sikes," he said into the mic.

"I'm not usually superstitious or afraid of the dark, but these woods have me creeped out." Her voice was strong and clear, disguising any fear she might be feeling.

"Know what you mean. I don't like the funnel it creates. If our guy wants to make a hit on me, now would be the time."

"Don't borrow trouble, Russell." Her words were tenser than before. "The trail is dangerous enough without someone chasing— Damn!"

Sam strained to hear what was going on with her. "You all right?" He waited for her response, his muscles bunching in his gut.

After what seemed an aeon, Kat's voice sounded in his headset. "I'm okay. I crashed my sled into a tree. There's some glacial buildup in the middle of a curve, I recommend slowing the team before you hit it."

"Thanks." Sam climbed another rise and the trail curved to the left, the trees dangerously close together. "Whoa!" He pressed the brake and slowed the team until they traversed the curve at little more than a snail's pace. His sled runners hit the icy patch but because they were going slow enough, he didn't slide far off the center of the curve before he was able to right it. "I owe you one, Sikes."

"Damn right you do."

"How much farther until you plan to stop?"

"I want to clear these trees. If I remember correctly, there's a flat swamp a little farther ahead. There's usually a camp set up around there for the front-runners."

Sam held tight to the handlebar and leaned into another turn. His legs tired and his back felt a little strained as he struggled to maneuver the twisting trail. "Good. I could use some food."

A loud crack sounded in front of him. With the dogs running as fast as they could through the trail, Sam didn't have time to react. A tree the size of a freight train crashed to the ground twenty feet ahead of Striker. Branches slammed into the lead and wheel dogs and the others skidded to a halt, bunching up until they were a pile of legs and tails.

"Whoa!" Sam pounded his boot into the brake, leaning all his weight into it. He tossed his snow hook into the snow, trying to slow the downward momentum, but the sled continued sliding toward the frightened dogs.

Not until the front runner of the sled touched the tail of Red, one of the swing dogs, did the three hundred pounds of supplies and equipment halt.

"What's going on?" Kat called into the headset.

"A tree." Sam leaped from the runners and ran around the sled, pulling dogs out of the pile, untangling necklines one dog at a time until he could reach the mess beneath the thick, spruce branches.

Dogs yelped and somewhere at the bottom of the heap he heard Striker whine. "I'm getting to you, boy. Hold on."

"Tree? What about a tree? Did you hit one? Are you okay? Is the team okay? Tell me something."

"A tree fell in front of my team. I'm digging them out now."

"A tree what?" A string of curses spewed from her mouth followed by a loud "Whoa!"

Sam unbuckled the wheel dogs, Rudy and Bear, from their necklines and they ran to the side, both unhurt.

In the minute amount of moonlight trickling through the remaining trees, Sam could make out Striker and Hammer struggling to free themselves from the nightmare of branches and lines. Striker whined and bit at the branch lying across his midsection.

"Hang on, boy. I'll get you out." Sam struggled to find a good place to stand and not put more pressure on the branch trapping both Striker and Hammer.

Hammer didn't make a noise, settling back against the snow.

Not good. If he were okay, he'd be fighting a lot harder to work his way free of the branch.

Sam reached through the branches and found the snap connecting the gangline to Striker's harness. He flicked it open then reached for Hammer's. The branch had caught Hammer across the left shoulder and had him pinned to the ground. Sam had to grope beneath the heavy branch to find the clip, but he couldn't reach it. After several attempts, he unfolded his pocketknife and cut the dog's harness.

He backed away and bent at the knees to lift the branch. It didn't move far with the weight of the tree pressing it against the ground. Muscles straining, Sam hefted, but the tree didn't budge. He raced back to the sled for his ax and went to work hacking away at the biggest branch that pressed the smaller ones into Hammer and Striker.

Sam swung the sharp ax into the branch, cutting his way through until the branch bounced up, no longer held down by the heavy tree trunk. Sam grabbed the thick limb and lifted it as high as he could, which only brought it up to his knees.

Striker wiggled and fought beneath the branch and eventually freed himself. Hammer was another story; he lay still, his tail slapping softly against the snow, a low whine coming from deep in his throat.

Sam had a dilemma. He couldn't hold the heavy branch up and pull the dog free at the same time. Nor could he drag it away or lower it again without causing more damage to Hammer.

Then Kat was there, leaping unsteadily through the snow, stepping around the dogs gathered around. She dived beneath the branch and half dragged, half lifted the dog out.

When all the animals were clear, Sam lowered the spruce branch, sinking to his knees in the snow. He hadn't realized just how heavy the tree was until the danger to the dogs was past. His arms shook as feeling slowly returned to his hands.

"He's hurt," Kat said beside him. "I can't tell how badly. Could be some internal bleeding or concussion. He needs a vet."

Sam moved across the snow and knelt beside her over Hammer's limp body. Despite his injuries, the dog's tail continued thumping against the snow. "That's right, you're a good boy." He stripped off his gloves and ran his hands over the animal's body, feeling for broken limbs and checking for any open wounds.

Hammer wasn't bleeding except for a couple minor scratches, but he didn't want to get up. A bad sign.

Sam lifted him into his arms and loaded him gently onto the sled, nestling him in between the straw and feed bag. Once he had the injured animal placed, he moved to untangle the rest of the tug-line and stretched it out to the side of the trail. He'd have to lead the team off the trail to get around the tree.

Kat was ahead of him, checking each dog and gathering loose booties from beneath the branches of the tree. "Striker seems okay so far, but I'd keep an eye on him. The rest are fine."

Dogs yipped farther along the trail.

"How far ahead were you?" Sam asked.

"About half a mile. I found a clearing wide enough to turn the team and headed back as soon as I could."

Sam hooked each dog into their positions along the tug-line, giving them the once-over again for good measure. They were excited and nervous, but they'd survive.

His heart swelled with pride. Alaskan huskies were born and bred to run. But they weren't invincible. A soft whine came from the sled.

Sam's lips tightened. When he had the last dog fastened in place, he grabbed a flashlight from his supplies and switched it on. Without a word, he tromped through the snow to the base of the spruce lying across the trail.

Kat followed close on his heals. "You think someone dumped this tree on purpose?"

"We'll find out."

He shone the beam on the trunk, following the length of it to the base. There were roots sticking out, but upon closer inspection, he saw that some of them had been severed. Recently. "Looks like this tree might have been leaning already, but someone gave it a little more reason to fall."

Chapter Five

Every time Kat looked back, she could see Hammer's head sticking out of the top of Sam's sled bag. The more she thought about the dog, the tree and its cut roots, the madder she got.

The Iditarod wasn't a race for sissies. With enough inherent dangers built into the rugged landscape and unforgiving weather, the addition of a saboteur made it unconscionably perilous.

Sam insisted she lead the way to the campsite. Thankfully, they only had another mile to go before the winding trail leveled out and descended gradually into a long, narrow frozen swamp. A cheerful campfire shone across the expanse.

Other contestants sat around the fire sipping from canteen cups, smiling and joking. Al Fendley sat in the middle, laughing louder than anyone, commanding center stage.

The man had the nerve to pound his chest like a Neanderthal and announce, "I'm going to win this race." He stared at Kat, daring the new arrival to re-fute his claim.

A seasoned veteran of the Iditarod, Evy Gray, laughed. "How can you be so sure you'll win?"

Al's eyes narrowed, his gaze fixed on Sam's sled en-tering the camp. "I like winning."

Evy tossed her coffee dregs into the snow. "You and everyone else out here."

Kat shook her head. So the man won one race in the past. That didn't mean he would win this one. Too many elements factored into the outcome. Even the best mushers were struck by misfortune. The moun-tains were tough on the teams and the sleds, but the bitter cold and debilitating wind blowing snow in from the coast was equally daunting. The best you could hope for was to arrive at the finish line with all your team intact.

Dogs were bedded down in nests of straw, some buried so deep all you could see were flashes of eyes blinking in the reflection of the firelight.

Kat grounded her snow hook and climbed off the runners, every muscle in her body screaming for a soft bed. The hard-packed snow and a warm sleeping bag would have to do. But she had at least an hour's worth of work to accomplish before she could claim her much-needed sleep. She also had a few questions for Sam. Questions that had been gnawing at her gut since the gunfire earlier that day. She had a feeling there was a lot more to Sam Russell than he let on.

Kat had loosened her bale of straw and let it fall to

the ground when the man prominent in her thoughts pulled his team in beside hers.

The dogs greeted each other with excited yips and wagging tails. Kat rounded her sled to Sam's. "How's Hammer?"

Sam untied his straw bale from the sled and let it fall. "Quiet, but holding his own. That tree knocked the stuffing out of him. I hope it didn't do much more damage than that."

Kat rubbed her gloved hand over the dog's snout. He whimpered, his tail drumming inside the waterproof sled bag. "Need help?"

"No thanks, I got it covered." He took half the bale and tromped through the snow, dropping flakes of straw beside each dog all the way up to Striker. There he kneeled and ran his hands over the lead. "Good boy." He was good with the dogs, ensuring their health above his own.

Kat admired a man who loved animals and took care of their needs first.

While Sam bedded down his dogs, Kat did the same with her team, managing a lot less straw at a time, but accomplishing the task as quickly and efficiently as possible. As soon as the huskies were fed and settled down for the night, she could eat and rest. Just the thought of food made her stomach rumble.

She surfaced the pan from inside her stash of supplies, filled it with snow and positioned it over her portable cooker. The dogs needed water and food. They could run an extended length of time as long as she kept them well fed and hydrated, resting them for as many hours as they'd been on the trail. She laid the dogs' bowls out and poured the bag of food into each before adding hot water.

As the dogs tore into their meal, she removed their booties. They didn't need them to sleep, just to run. The booties were protection against the snow clumping up between their pads. One at a time, she rubbed soothing ointment into their paws and massaged their shoulders and wrists.

By the time she finished feeding and caring for her team, Kat grabbed her sleeping bag and a small plastic bag of stew Paul had packed with her food drop. She'd already thawed it in the water she'd used to feed and water the dogs. Tired to the bone, she didn't have the energy to lay out her sleeping bag, much less feed herself. But if she wanted to make it to Nome, she had to keep up her strength, as well as that of her team. Sam had been right. She might be in good physical shape, but she hadn't been training with the dogs. There were muscles she'd forgotten about that were now screaming in her hands, arms and shoulders.

Sam had finished with his team well ahead of her. He'd used the remaining straw to create a cushioned area large enough for two sleeping bags and close to the campfire someone had built.

Despite how cold and tired she was, her pulse quickened. The thought of lying so close to Sam warmed her blood all the way to her frozen toes. No, she preferred to believe the warmth was due to the fact she was now standing next to the roaring fire. A fire that felt too good. She pushed the hood of her parka off, pulled off her goggles and slid the wool-lined cap from her head. God, it felt good for her head to breathe. She'd forgotten how confining all the clothing could be and wanted to shed a few layers. Kat grabbed the tip of a glove with her teeth and removed one, then the other. The cold bit at her ears and fingertips, the fire warming only the side she exposed to the heat.

Fendley and the others had drifted off to their sleeping bags for a few necessary hours of sleep. Those still awake worked toward getting to sleep as quickly as possible.

"You can have the other half of the straw," Sam said, jerking his head toward the cozy bed he'd constructed.

"No...thanks." No way. The thought of being with another man made her feel unfaithful to Marty's memory, even as she gazed longingly at the straw, her sleeping bag still held tightly in her arms.

"I'm just offering you a warmer place to lie down than the snow, since you used all your straw on the dogs." He shrugged. "Take it or leave it."

He dug into the plastic bag filled with frozen stew, his attention not so much on her as the food.

The man wasn't interested in her, he was just being nice. Internally calling herself all kinds of a fool for the direction her thoughts had taken, Kat accepted Sam's offer and tossed her sleeping bag on the straw, plunking down next to him. Her stomach growled so loudly, surely everyone in camp heard it. Kat was too hungry to be embarrassed, and she tucked into Paul's stew.

A comfortable silence lengthened between them that

Kat wasn't sure she should be so comfortable with. "Who do you think cut that tree?" she said after a few minutes.

"I would venture to guess the same guy who shot at me earlier."

"Maybe we should go back over the probable suspects. I can't imagine many of the folks who have you on their hit list would venture out on the Iditarod voluntarily just to kill you." Kat licked her spoon, glancing over at Sam as she did. "Hopefully he won't last long in these conditions and he's forced to head back. The weather is too cold for most to stomach for long."

"This guy was a professional sniper or at least someone who knows how to handle a gun. A hunter." Sam poured hot water from the pan in his cooker into his canteen cup and stirred in the instant coffee he'd brought with him. The welcome aroma filled the frigid air, a cloud of steam rising from the dark brew. "If he really wanted me dead, he wouldn't have missed the first time. Unless…" He sipped from the cup.

"Unless?"

"Unless he didn't want to kill me yet." He stared at Kat over the rim of his cup as he swallowed another sip.

She bit. "Why would he wait?"

"Maybe he doesn't have me where he wants me." He set the cup away from his lips. "Perhaps he wants to scare me into quitting the race. Or maybe he just wanted to play with me before he kills me." His words were conversational, as if he were talking about the latest movie he'd seen, not someone shooting at him.

Kat stared at Sam as if he'd grown horns. She just

didn't understand how he could be so nonchalant. "Who would play games like that?"

Sam's eye narrowed as he stared into the flames. "If it's someone after me because of my work, it could be anyone from the state of Alaska. How many hit men do you know from the lower forty-eight who would come up to Alaska just to play cat and mouse with his target?"

"A really sick killer if you ask me." A chill that had nothing to do with the cold slithered down Kat's spine. She'd been in deadly situations as an S.O.S. agent, but she'd usually known who her enemy was. Out here, she hadn't even seen him. All she knew was that he had a snowmobile and a high-powered rifle. He might even have a chain saw or handsaw stashed somewhere, based on the clean cut at the roots of the tree.

Sam sipped more coffee. "Not many men would be willing to come this far north. It would have to be someone experienced in arctic conditions."

"So we're back to someone from Alaska. Someone who would know the trail and the route the Iditarod takes. You don't suppose someone in the race has a contract out on you to keep you from winning, do you?" Her gaze wandered over to the sleeping bag where Al Fendley lay snuggled so deeply all she could see was the tip of his nose and the reflection of the firelight shining off his open eyes. Eyes staring directly at her.

Had he heard them talking?

No, that was absurd. She and Sam were talking in low tones audible only to those a foot or two away from them, not six yards. Angry at how her imagination conjured enemies where none existed before, she downed a large swig of coffee, sputtering as it burned its way down her throat. Served her right.

Sam pounded her back. "You okay?"

"I'm fine." She shook his hand free, afraid she could get used to him touching her. Instead, she faced him, schooling her face and emotions into an unreadable mask. "Talk to me, Sam. Tell me everything in your past that could lead to an assassin landing on your tail. You might start with your military training."

Sam's eyes widened for a brief second.

If Kat hadn't been watching she would have missed that little flash of surprise.

His gaze dropped to the remaining liquid in his cup. "What makes you think I've had military training?"

"Don't bullshit me, Russell. You've had military training. It was obvious in the way you moved when you were under fire. If it wasn't military, it was SWAT or something equally dangerous, requiring live-fire training."

The silence lengthened between them. For a moment, Kat didn't think Sam would answer.

"I went into the army straight out of high school."

"So? That explains a little of it, but not all. Every soldier receives basic techniques in fighting. You moved more like a professional soldier, Special Forces or something."

He stared at her for a moment, his lip curling on one edge. "Busted. I was in the Special Forces."

"Now we're getting somewhere." Kat took one last sip from her canteen and yawned. "Let's get settled in and you can fill me in on the rest."

He didn't answer, just stood and extended a hand to her.

When their fingers touched, a jolt of energy ran the length of her arm. She hadn't had that kind of reaction to a man's touch since…

Kat jerked her hand free and reached for her pan, burning her palm on the handle. "Damn." The handle had left an angry red welt across her right hand. Great, she had to use that palm to hold on to the handlebar. The race would be long and painful with a burn just where the welt lay.

"Let me see that." Sam grabbed her hand in one of his and, with the other, scooped a handful of snow from the ground, forming it into a small ball. "Be careful. You can't eliminate my competition so early. It takes the fun out of the race."

For a big man, his touch was surprisingly gentle.

When Kat tried to tug her hand free of his, he held firm. "I won't bite. The cold will help take the sting out of the burn." He pressed the icy clump to her open palm. For a long moment, he gently rubbed the snowball across her palm.

Instead of cooling her, the movement caused her blood to heat and race throughout her body, warming her insides all the way to her cramping toes.

She stared at his hand holding the snow, afraid to look up into his eyes. More afraid of what she'd reveal in her own. She wasn't ready to let another man close. Especially this one. He spelled danger.

Sam cleared his throat then asked, "That feel better?"

Kat pulled her hand away and wiped it down the side

of her pants. "Much." And worse. She grabbed her rolled-up sleeping bag and untied the cords, flicking it open across the straw.

Sam stretched his next to hers and they bumped shoulders.

This wasn't going to work. Kat knew that with a certainty. She bent to retrieve her bag, but Sam got to it before she could.

He dropped to his own bag and unzipped the edge of hers before he glanced up. "If you'll take off your boots, I'll put them by the fire to dry."

Kat hesitated. The urge to run struck her so hard she almost jumped back on the trail to find a quieter, solitary place she wouldn't have to share with anyone, especially Sam Russell. But she was here to help protect him. Not to mention fatigue overcame fear and she sank onto the cushioned sleeping bag, reaching out to unlace her boots.

While she untied the lace and loosened the one-pull set, Sam grabbed the other and worked the bow and knots out. Thanks to the waterproof exterior, her boots remained dry, except for her own perspiration. She pulled the liner to the top and handed her boot to Sam.

As Sam placed the boots next to the fire, Kat crawled into the sleeping bag and zipped it to her chin. She'd duck completely inside before she fell asleep, but she wanted to know more about this man her brother had felt so sure about, he'd allowed him to move into their home.

One yawn led to another and she pressed her hand to her mouth.

"Get some sleep." Sam pulled his boots off and

placed them next to hers by the fire. Side by side, as if they belonged.

"No." Another jaw-splitting yawn overcame her and she laughed at the end. "I'm tired, but determined."

"I noticed that about you." Sam slid into his bag and zipped it up to his chest. He turned on his side and propped himself on his elbow to stare at her. "What are you determined about, besides winning?" He smiled, the gesture softening the hard planes of his face.

"You." She yawned, her eyes heavy. "I want to know more about you."

The smile slipped and he glanced toward the fire. "What do you want to know?"

"How long you've lived in Alaska, for starters." Kat rolled to face him. Her face warmed—and not from the heat of the fire.

"I've lived here four years."

"And before that?"

"Virginia." The word was clipped and didn't invite further questioning, as if that one word was all he was willing to share. "What about you?"

Kat's eyes widened. "I thought you knew all about me. You've lived with my brother for a year."

"I know about your childhood from Paul's accounts. Let's see, you used to tag along behind him and make him crazy and you nagged him into going to college. You slept in the dog kennels many nights when one of your dogs was sick. I know that you lost your father when you both were young, and that Vic was more or less a surrogate parent to you."

Kat laughed. "Paul talks more than a girl."

"Paul talks about the things he cares about." Sam's eyes narrowed. "What do you do in D.C.?"

Although used to people asking her this question, when it came from Sam, Kat wasn't prepared with her canned answer. She hesitated for a long moment, the urge to tell him the truth hovering on her lips. What was it about the man that made her want to open up? Whatever it was, it wasn't her right to tell him certain things about herself. When she'd signed on to S.O.S., she'd agreed to never tell anyone outside the organization what exactly she did. Each agent was given the company response "I'm in security." Only that response stuck in her throat and all she could say was, "I work for the government."

"That could mean one of two things. Either you're bored with your job, or your work is classified and if you told me, you'd have to kill me." Sam's smile slid across his face again.

Kat could get used to his smile all too easily. "I could say the same about your answer. Although as far as vague goes, you had me beat." Her brows rose high on her forehead. "When you were in Virginia, were you in the army then?"

"No."

Boy, he wasn't going to give her any more than she gave him. If she wanted answers she'd have to ask the right questions. "Did *you* work with the government?"

"You could say I did."

That was more than she'd expected, but still not

enough. "Did you make someone mad while you were living in Virginia?"

"Doesn't everyone make someone mad at some time or another?"

"You're avoiding the question." Kat frowned. "I'm trying to determine whether or not your past has risen to bite you in the butt."

"I started over when I moved to Alaska. Anything happening now would have to be from my affiliations while I've lived in this state."

The door to his past in Virginia had been firmly shut in her face. "Now we're getting somewhere."

It was Sam's turn to frown. "What do you mean by that?"

"A lot of people come to Alaska for the same reasons pioneers left their homes during the 1800s. It's a chance to escape persecution and hard times. A chance to start over."

"Don't go making more of my comments than what's there." Sam turned onto his back and stared up at the stars. "It's time to sleep."

"No way. You have to tell me what you were running away from."

"I don't have to tell you anything." He rolled over, giving her his back. "I *do* have to get some sleep. We need to be on the trail in less than three hours. I suggest you get some sleep, too."

"Fine." She'd let him run now, but sooner or later, she'd find out why he'd left his world behind and escaped to Alaska to start over.

Kat lay back in her sleeping bag and gazed up at the stars, a thrill of excitement coursing through her veins. She'd struck a nerve with Sam, and it had forged a crack in his armor. A crack maybe he didn't even recognize yet. With a little more persistence, she'd figure out what it was that had made him feel the need to get away.

What were some of the reasons men left the lower forty-eight to come to Alaska? Some had hit rock bottom financially and wanted to start over as far away from those who'd known them in the past, including creditors. Others had committed crimes they didn't want to get caught for. Some were recovering from broken relationships. Her pulse slowed and her breath caught in her throat. What if Sam's reason had been a woman?

Kat cast a glance toward him, but all she could see was the back of his sleeping bag. Had Sam given up his job and his home to move to Alaska because of a failed relationship?

Depressing thought. Although why it should depress her, she didn't know. But it did.

You're a fool.

Her mind spun in a thousand different directions, trying to piece together the minimal amount of information. The more she thought about Sam, the more confused she became until her tired body forced her brain to slow. As she drifted into a light sleep, her last thought was of Royce's words. "Sam can handle it." Oh, yeah, she was sure Sam could handle most anything. But why did Royce know that?

SLEEP ELUDED SAM when he needed it most. Even as the sound of Kat's slow, steady breathing carried through the crisp night air, he remained alert for any further attempts on his life. Perhaps having Kat so close to him wasn't a good idea after all. If the sniper decided to take another shot at him, he might get Kat instead.

More than thoughts of the sniper kept him awake. Kat's questions and comments had struck too close to home. He still didn't know if she worked for S.O.S. In some ways it would be much better if she did. Then he could admit that he'd worked for them, too, in his past life. But that would open him up to questions he didn't want to answer. Like, why did you quit?

His last mission had ended his career as an agent. Not that Royce blamed him for what had happened. Sam blamed himself. If he'd been more in tune with the job at hand and less enamored of the danger and excitement, he might have seen through his partner's lies.

Second-guessing had never gotten him anywhere. Bradley English had fooled all of them and his deception had cost the life of a young Saudi princess. Sam blamed himself for the loss of the child, an innocent caught in the cross fire. When her doting Saudi grandfather captured Bradley, Sam had no choice but to walk away. The man had been laundering money to terrorists bent on punishing Americans and anybody who openly supported American ideals. One of his business deals ended in gunfire and mortars. The little princess had been collateral damage.

When the smoke cleared and his partner had been left

in the hands of the Saudi government, Sam came home, awash with his failure. He'd gone to Saudi Arabia with the intention of finding and stopping the American responsible for funding an attack on major cities in the United States. He'd never captured the ringleader. Instead he'd lost his partner to the wrong side.

He'd also lost his stomach for the job and his heart for the work he'd loved. Even before Royce had called him into his office, Sam had made his decision to leave the S.O.S. and ultimately D.C. Although Royce tried to talk him out of it, Sam had remained firm.

When he'd left his home in Virginia, he'd cut all ties to his life as an S.O.S. agent. The scars and the guilt ran deep and he couldn't bear the constant reminder. Even Sam's relationship with Leanne had been collateral damage.

Sam wondered what had become of Bradley, a man he'd once mistakenly called friend. Had he been tortured and executed? The U.S. government wouldn't have done anything to save him from his fate. For one, if the Saudi government had known both he and Sam had been sent by the U.S., the incident would have created an international firestorm of accusations and sanctions. With the nature of S.O.S. agents, the less anyone knew about them, the better.

Still, Sam wondered.

Had Bradley survived, would he have hated Sam for leaving him behind? Would he have blamed him for allowing the Saudi government to mete out their own form of punishment on a man who'd caused the death of a small princess?

Not that it mattered. Bradley English was either dead or locked up in a hellish Saudi prison paying for what he'd done. Sam couldn't feel sorry for a man who'd betrayed his country.

He must have fallen asleep, because the frantic sound of dogs barking woke him with a start. He reached for his gun as he rolled to his belly in his sleeping bag.

Kat sat up, fighting her sleeping-bag zipper. "What's happening?"

With the pale light of morning still hours away, clouds had covered the stars and a light snow fell over the camp. Sam scanned the vicinity in the light from the dying fire.

The dogs were going nuts, barking like crazed creatures.

When Sam spotted the object of their concern, he quietly reached for his boots. "Stay down!" he shouted to the people stirring in their sleeping bags.

A bull moose the size of a truck stood in the middle of the camp, quietly sniffing through the contents of one sled.

"Hey, that's my sled. Get the hell out!" a musher called.

Sam recognized Al Fendley, as loud and obnoxious in the morning as he had been the night before.

The moose's head rose and he stared at Al.

The man shut up and sank low to the ground, scrambling for his boots.

Sam had his boots on and his gun cocked, waiting for

the moose to make his move. Hopefully, it was the move to leave the camp without harming anyone. If not, Sam would provide a little encouragement to make him leave.

Every musher in the camp was wide-awake by now, yelling and waving in an attempt to scare the moose away.

When Sam raised his gun, Kat put out her hand. "Be careful. A bull moose can be unpredictable. What might scare one will only anger another."

"Trust me. I won't do something stupid." He panned the area. Mushers who'd been sleeping in the area behind the moose gathered their boots and sought cover beneath nearby trees.

Al Fendley had his boots on and had apparently decided to forgo lacing them for beating a hasty retreat to a nearby tree. As soon as he stood, the moose's head lowered.

"Get down, Al!" Kat called out.

Al gave the moose one last look then dashed for the cover of a tree twenty feet away.

"Not good," Kat muttered. "That moose is going to—"

Chapter Six

Dogs yelped and dodged out of the way of twelve hundred pounds of angry, charging moose.

Al screamed like a woman and ran faster.

If the situation weren't a life-or-death state of affairs for all the mushers and their dogs in the camp, Kat might have laughed at Al's scream. She might be screaming, too, if she was the object of the bull moose's ire.

Sam aimed his gun high over the top of the moose's head and squeezed off a round.

The loud bang made the moose's stride stutter, but he kept charging.

Sam fired again.

Kat held her breath. If the bullets struck the beast they might hurt it a little, but most likely make him even angrier. An angry moose in a camp full of dogs and people could prove deadly.

Apparently Sam understood the dangers, as well. His bullets flew over the top of the moose, missing him completely.

This time, the sound of the gunshot made the moose jump and spin in a complete circle as if he was looking for the source of the loud noise. His eyes flared, wide and wild.

Sam fired another round and the moose veered toward the tree line, leaping over teams, plowing through empty sleeping bags and snow-covered piles of fallen trees.

Not until the moose had disappeared into the darkness and the sound of his hooves crashing through the underbrush faded, did the mushers come out of hiding. And then it was to hurry through their predawn routine, anxious to get back on the trail in the event the moose decided to return to wreak even more havoc.

Without a word, Kat slipped into her boots and rolled her sleeping bag into a tight bundle. Once she'd stowed it in her sled bag, she reached for her pan and filled it with snow to melt.

While the dogs tucked into their breakfast, she made coffee. Then with a bagful of booties in her hand, she fitted fresh new booties to each dog's feet, ensuring they were tied snugly without cutting off the circulation to provide maximum protection to the dog's paws.

Now that the danger was over, the mushers were talking and laughing. One by one they returned to the trail, continuing their push to complete the race.

"You get enough rest?" Sam asked.

"Plenty." One of the things you accepted as a musher was the understanding that you didn't get much sleep during the race. You could always sleep when you made it to the finish line. Four hours and a hot cup of coffee was all she required to give her the burst of energy she needed to keep going. "How's Hammer?"

"Looking a little more himself. He'll be hard to keep on the sled today, but I'm not letting him race. I'll drop him at the Finger Lake checkpoint."

Kat nodded. It was the right thing to do. Even if the dog looked as if he could continue the race, he'd be better off sent back to Anchorage where prison inmates would care for him until Paul could get over there to claim the dog.

Sam finished his coffee and pulled a bag of beef jerky from his supplies. He handed her a strand of the chewy meat. "Eat this."

She shook her head. "I'm not hungry."

"You need to keep up your strength. I can't have you letting down your brother because you refused to eat a healthy breakfast."

She couldn't help smiling. "You call that healthy?"

"Better than nothing." He bit off a hunk.

"I had coffee."

"Although some consider coffee breakfast food, it lacks protein." He glared at her with a twinkle in his eye. "Eat."

Kat liked the light teasing and the fact that Sam cared enough about her health to force her to eat. She grabbed the jerky and tried to bite off a piece, struggling for a moment before she accomplished the task. She pulled her snow hook from the ground, still chewing on the salty meat. When she called out, "Let's go!" to her team, it sounded as if she had a golf ball in her mouth. But the dogs were happy to give her garbled words the correct interpretation and they took off. With one foot on a runner, Kat used the other to angle the sled onto the trail, leaving the camp behind.

The light snow grew heavier, the flakes fat and wet, slapping against Kat's goggles and coating the scarf over her mouth. The trail was tricky through the wooded area and she had to use her headlamp to see since the clouds covered the stars. Morning hadn't arrived in Alaska. They'd be almost to Finger Lake before it did.

All her concentration centered on negotiating the trail through trees, across swamps and smaller lakes until the team reached Onestone Lake. The large rock in the center of the lake was a welcome sight, indicating the tricky path of this run lay behind them.

"You makin' it all right back there, Russell?" For the past hour, she'd been quiet, needing all her concentration for the darkened trail.

"We're holding our own." His resonant voice warmed her insides.

"No signs of our sniper?"

"None, so far."

"Good, maybe he's called it quits with the snow coming down harder."

"I'm not counting on it." His previously warm voice turned colder, more forbidding. "And don't you let your guard down for a minute."

"I hadn't planned on it." Her shoulders ached with the effort of holding the handlebar and the tension of wondering when and where their pursuer might attack again. She really hoped he'd given up, but like Sam, she wouldn't count on it, either. Kat removed one hand from the handlebar and flexed her arm. The sled hit a bump beneath the light layer of snow. Her hand clamped back down on the handlebar and she leaned into the runner to keep the sled on course.

"Hey, Sikes, who do you really work for in D.C.?"

Her sled skidded sideways on another hidden ridge, buying Kat a little time to think of an answer. When she was fully in control, she responded, "I told you, I work for the government."

"I know D.C. is a big place, but did you ever run into a guy by the name of Royce Fontaine?"

Kat's breath caught in her throat. Tazer was right. Sam knew Royce. "I met a lot of people in D.C. What does he look like?"

"Never mind."

Let him have a taste of Twenty Questions. "So, Sam, have you always been in oil?"

"No."

Sheesh, getting answers from this guy was like pulling teeth with a string. But then what did she expect. S.O.S. agents didn't just blurt out a full job description and information about the cases they handled. She chuckled at the thought.

"What's so funny?" Again his voice warmed her all over, even her fingers going numb on the handlebar.

"Oh, nothing," she said airily, a smile lifting the corners of her mouth behind her wool scarf.

"So do you know Royce or not?"

"Maybe."

"That's not an answer." He paused for a long moment. "But I get it."

"I bet you do." That Sam understood the need for secrecy didn't stop that twisted feeling in Kat's gut. Sam had worked for the S.O.S. A thousand more questions raced through her mind. About that time she hit another bump in the trail and she righted her sled, her palm stinging where she'd burned it the night before.

"How long?" she asked.

"How long what?"

"How long have you known Royce?"

"Eight years." His words were clipped. He obviously didn't want to talk about it.

Kat had worked with Royce for three years. Before Marty died, she couldn't imagine working anywhere else. She loved serving her country and she loved the excitement and danger inherent in the job. But the danger had taken its toll in the form of her husband. Reality had knocked hard at her door and made her reevaluate her commitment. She still loved the S.O.S. and the people working there, but she wasn't sure she still had it in her to wait around for the next person to die.

"Why did you leave D.C.?" she pushed.

He didn't answer and for a moment, she thought maybe the radio was defective. "Are you there?"

Sam sighed. "I'm here. The reasons I left are personal."

"I can respect your desire to keep your reasons to yourself, but we have some idiot out there determined to make this your last race."

"I understand. The guy that influenced my decision couldn't be out here. He's out of action."

Oh, so that was it. Someone had died. A partner, one of his targeted assignments? Kat wasn't so sure she wanted to know. If the person was dead, what difference did it make to the current situation?

None.

An idea occurred to her and she switched her mic off so that Sam couldn't hear her. Digging her satellite phone out of her pocket, she connected to Tazer.

Before Kat could say a word, Tazer said, "Oh, good, it's you."

"What's up?"

"You know when Royce said Sam could handle whatever?"

"Yes."

"I did some digging and questioning and found out that our Alaskan fantasy man used to be an S.O.S. agent. I pinned Royce with some pertinent questions and he owned up to it."

"I know."

"You know?" Tazer's surprise was evident even though her well-modulated tones did a fairly good job of hiding it. Kat knew Tazer.

"Yes, I figured it out. What I want to know is why he left. Would you get back to Royce and find out why Sam quit?"

"No can do, girl. When I pushed Royce with that very question, he shut me off. Said to stay out of it and leave Sam alone. It wasn't important."

"That's pretty cold for Royce."

Tazer huffed. "You're telling me."

"Wonder what the two of them know that's so all-fired secret they can't tell us."

"I don't know, but I'm not giving up yet. I still have my ace up my sleeve."

Kat thought for a moment. "Valdez?"

"The man's been here long enough to know Sam and, given the right motivation by yours truly, he'll sing."

Kat laughed. "If anyone can talk information out of a man, it's you, Tazer. Let me know what you find."

"You bet. You haven't had any more gunfire, have you?"

"No, but we almost got bulldozed by a bull moose early this morning."

"Honey, better you than me. I'll stick to my urban jungle. I can handle the animals there."

Kat laughed. "No guts, no glory."

"Then color me gutless."

"You're the bravest woman I know."

"Don't confuse bravery with stupidity," Tazer responded softly. "I think you're the bravest woman I know."

A lump lodged in Kat's throat and tears swam in her eyes, blurring her vision. "Then why don't I feel so brave?"

"But look at where you are," Tazer insisted. "You're on the Iditarod, for chrissakes. I wouldn't last two minutes out there, much less two weeks."

"It's not so bad." The sled bumped hard and she was forced to grab the handlebar with the hand holding the satellite phone. When she managed to regain her stability, she set the phone to her ear. "You still there?"

"Yeah."

"Look, if you hear anything else about Sam, let me know. Right now I need to hold on or I'll be sledless and my team will go on to Nome without me."

"Catch ya later. Be careful."

The sun had risen behind the heavy layer of clouds. At least the weak daylight made navigating the trail less treacherous.

Kat's earpiece hummed with the sound of Sam's voice. "You still with me?"

Kat switched on her mic. "I'm here."

"Want to stop at Finger Lake Lodge for a quick breakfast?"

"Sounds better than beef jerky, but no. I'd rather skip the media circus and stop farther down the trail so the gang won't be distracted."

With most of her attention on the trail, Kat cast glances over her shoulder when she came to long clear stretches. She wanted to keep Sam within watching range. If something happened and he couldn't tell her over the radio, she'd know within minutes to go looking for him. She just hoped nothing happened. Since yesterday's shooting, she hadn't heard the sound of a snowmobile following them. She prayed it would stay that way.

FINGER LAKE WAS just as much of a zoo as Kat predicted. With the runway only yards away from the dog-parking area, the checkpoint wasn't conducive to resting dogs.

Race officials didn't waste time checking Kat and Sam through and within a matter of minutes, they were on their way again.

The flakes fell heavier, layering the ground in thick white powder. Since the snow was fresh, it hadn't had time to settle and the few sleds in front of Kat and Sam hadn't packed it down. Six inches of powder came to the bellies of the dogs, slowing them and making their run more like a hopping routine through the heavy drifts. That kind of work would tire them quickly.

The winds were calm, leaving the snowfall undisturbed. For once, Sam wished for the biting wind to blow the trails clean of the freshly fallen snow. At least then he could see the hazards, the hidden brush, and hard ridges caused by snowmobile tracks.

His hands gripped the handlebar as they climbed over the ridge above the lodge at Finger Lake, leaving civilization and the imported-espresso stand behind. As he negotiated sharp twists in the narrow trails and dropped onto the south side of Red Lake, he breathed a sigh of relief. Although not nearly as treacherous as coming down off the hillsides, the lake had beaver dams hidden beneath the snow. If the dogs weren't careful, they could break a leg. If Sam wasn't watchful, he could break his sled.

"In all your travels, have you found a place as beautiful as Alaska?" Kat spoke softly and reverently into his ear, the sound sending a warm shiver across his skin.

"Never." Sam didn't hesitate. The beauty was unbeatable. He may have come to Alaska to escape his past, but he'd found the one place on earth he'd rather be. Ever-greens drooped with the weight of newfallen snow. Besides having worked for the same agency, he and Kat had something else in common—love of this land.

"I'm going to stop now to snack the guys." Ahead, Kat slowed to a halt near the tree line.

Sam pulled his team in beside hers. The dogs greeted as if they hadn't seen each other in days, never mind it had only been half an hour since they'd stopped at the Finger Lake checkpoint.

Kat had already unpacked her pans and started laying out the twigs and sticks she used to keep the cooker and pan from melting a hole in the snow and sinking. She worked with quiet efficiency until all the dog dishes were full and distributed. Not until then did she think about herself. She knew what was important and took care of others first. A nurturer, despite her tough demeanor during the shooting yesterday. A good agent to have on his side. Not a two-faced liar ready to sell his soul to the devil for a few dollars and the price of a child's life.

If Sam had teamed up with Kat at the agency, the mission might have turned out differently. But Kat hadn't been an S.O.S. agent back then. What had she done before S.O.S.? Royce didn't hire new agents with no prior combat, investigation or law-enforcement experience. He made a mental note to learn more.

Sam scooped snow into a pan and brought it to a boil, thawing two bags full of scrambled eggs and ham at the same time. He mixed hot water with the dog food to give the huskies a warm, nutritious meal, and scooped more snow to boil for coffee.

Kat wandered off to take care of business. When she returned, he handed her a small bag. "Mmm. Ham and eggs?" She dug in, scarfing down the food so fast she barely had time to swallow, much less taste it.

Sam smiled as he ate his meal at a more leisurely pace. "Paul and I spent days preparing the food and freezing it so that we'd have decent meals."

She glanced up over the top of her bag, a rosy blush rising in her cheeks. "Then I owe you and my brother a big thank-you. I get to reap the benefits of someone else's cooking."

"Paul said you weren't much use in the kitchen."

"More's the shame, because I love to eat." She shrugged. "Never liked cooking. I've eaten every kind of carryout ever invented. Thank goodness Paul had some talent with the pots and pans. He can make a mean stew and chili. What about you?"

"I can find my way around." He didn't tell her how much he loved cooking and experimenting with different recipes. "Only I don't like cooking for just me. Cooking is a task to be enjoyed with another."

"Anytime you want to experiment on a recipe, I'm your girl. I do wash dishes." She finished off her ham and eggs and leaned back against a tree.

The dogs stretched out on the snow, full and happily resting.

"Why don't you take a nap, I'll keep watch." Sam took her fork and the empty plastic bag. "I'll clean up."

"No, it's okay, I'm not tired." She yawned and laughed all at once. "Okay, maybe a minute or two. But I still have a race to win. Don't think I won't." She yawned again and closed her eyes.

Sam reached out and tugged her parka up over her head.

"Why'd you do that?" She blinked up at him. "I could have done that."

"I wanted to." He was so close he couldn't help himself. Leaning just a little closer, he pressed a kiss to her nose. "I'm glad you're on the trip with me."

"Good thing I'm not Paul. He might not be so understanding about being kissed." Her words faded off and she was asleep.

Sam smiled down at Kat, bundled in a powder-blue jacket and matching pants. Why then did he feel a surge of desire coursing through his veins? He could only imagine the curve of her breasts, the indentation of her waist and the well-defined, taut muscles of her thighs. He'd seen her moving from her bedroom to the bathroom back at the house near Anchorage in nothing more than a long nightshirt. Enough to cover all the necessary parts, but not to keep his imagination from running rampant.

With her midnight-black lashes brushing across her cheeks she looked more like a sleeping angel than a secret agent, and he was tempted to kiss more than her nose.

If he was smart, he'd pack her off and send her back to Anchorage. Hell, he'd be smart to pack himself off and head back. With a lunatic shooting at him and sabotaging the trail, he should drop from the race and head home.

Home. And where was that? Sam didn't have a place to call home. The room he rented from Paul had been the closest to a home he'd had in over a decade.

Kat had come back to Alaska because it was her home. She'd been born and raised in this rugged country. But was she back for a vacation? Or had she quit the S.O.S. like he had?

If she stayed in Alaska after the race, would she want Sam to move out? He didn't really want to cause a rift between Paul and his sister or be a third wheel in a tight-knit family unit.

Sam glanced around the white, snow-covered landscape. The silence was complete. The teams were bedded down and resting. He could even hear Kat snoring quietly.

The stress of the past couple of days settled over him and his eyelids pressed downward. Fifteen minutes of sleep wouldn't hurt him. The early morning moose hadn't given him all the sleep he'd hoped for. Sam settled back against the tree next to Kat and let his eyes close.

How long he slept, he didn't know, but the distant whine of a motor drifted through his subconscious and jerked him awake.

Sam jumped to his feet and panned the hillside. The snow had stopped, but he, Kat and the dogs were covered in a thin layer of the powder.

"What?" Kat lurched to her feet beside him, instantly awake. "Did you hear something?"

"I think I heard a snowmobile."

"Could be one of the spectators machining through the trails out from Finger Lake."

"Or it could be our sniper." He glanced at his watch then gathered the pans and stashed the trash in his sled. "We'd better get moving. We've been here for over two hours."

The dogs were up and dancing around, ready to run.

Kat and Sam checked the lines and booties. Before too long, they were back on the trail facing some of the toughest terrain yet.

"I'd like to make Rainy Pass before dark." Sam tugged at the tie-down straps one last time before stepping behind his sled.

Kat stood waiting. "Me, too. There are some really ugly side-hill trails I don't want to negotiate in the dark."

"Exactly." Sam inhaled a long steady breath. "Ready?"

"As ready as I'll ever be." She grinned and pulled her goggles down over her eyes and her wool scarf up over her mouth.

Sam adjusted his headset and spoke into the mic. "I'll take the lead. Stay close."

"You got it, but I'm still winning this race." The light banter belied the nervous quiver in her voice.

They had some of the worst trail conditions just ahead. Any musher worth his salt would be afraid. Sam was no different. He remembered this leg from last year when he'd almost skidded down a hill sideways and dumped his sled twice. The danger was part and parcel

of the entire Iditarod experience. A musher being followed by a psychotic man on a snowmobile only added
to the level of anxiety building in Sam.

But staying in one place wasn't going to get him
through this race.

TWO DAYS ON the Iditarod. After the snow stopped, the
temperatures dipped below minus twenty. The dogs
liked it cold. Too warm and they had to rest during the
heat of the day. The cool air stung her cheeks where the
scarf didn't cover her skin. She welcomed the stinging
to help her wake up the rest of the way.

Groggy didn't make for good trail riding. Kat shook
her head, content to watch the man ahead of her. Had
he really kissed her nose as she fell asleep, or had that
been wishful thinking? And where did she get off with
wishful thinking? Marty had been all the man she'd
needed in her life.

Marty's gone. The cold voice of reason failed to
warm her.

That old empty feeling that usually hit her square in
the gut didn't hit her so hard this time. Was she finally
getting over him? Had coming home to Alaska helped her
see that she still had a life beyond her husband's death?

They'd been climbing steadily, winding and turning
through narrow trails following a ravine. At the top of
the ravine, the trail ran west along the southern slope of
a ridge. The teams raced through areas of frozen swamps
alternating with twisting trails through timber growths.
They ran along the forested benches on the lower slope

of a five-thousand-foot ridge, the quiet and deadly sentinel of the entrance to Ptarmigan and Rainy Passes.

If their shooter knew anything about the Iditarod, he'd figure out the best place to inflict the most damage wouldn't be on the side-hill trails of Happy Valley. He'd wait until Sam reached Dalzell Gorge to do his damage. Not that the trail wasn't dangerous here in Happy Valley.

Kat couldn't see Sam. The trail wound too tightly in and out of trees and around rock formations. "When you see the yellow signs that say Dangerous Trail Conditions Ahead and Watch your Ass! slow down."

"I know." His words were tight, clipped. "There it is. Take it easy."

"I will." She chuckled. "It's you I'm worried about."

"Well, here goes nothing. See ya at the bottom of Happy Valley Canyon."

Chapter Seven

The trail dropped down, twisting through the trees. Thanks to the heavy snow of earlier that day, Sam's sled moved slower and didn't skid off the path. Then the trail vanished.

He was ready for it, he'd remembered it from the last time he'd run this race. His heart jumped to his throat as the team disappeared over the edge, two at a time. The last to take the plunge, the swing dogs pulled the sled over the edge of the cliff.

Sam clung to the handlebar as the back of the sled tipped high into the air before rocketing downward.

The small cliff marked the entrance to the Happy River Steps. Sam pressed all his weight into the foot brake. The trail veered to the left and Sam's runners settled into the ruts left by the contestants before him. He leaned his sled almost on its side, the downhill runner in the air, the bulk of the sled hugging the uphill slope. At the bottom of the incline, the trail swung back to the right to cross the slope again.

Just as he headed out across the side-hill trail, a loud crack rent the air, followed by another just like it.

Sam's white-knuckled grip tightened on the handlebar.

"What the hell was that?" Kat called out.

He knew that sound and it had no business on a snow-covered slope. Not here. Not now. "Gunfire."

"If you're on the slope, get the hell off! Find cover," Kat called.

Another shot rang out, hitting the corner of his sled bag. Sam couldn't go any faster or he risked sliding off the trail and over the fifty-foot cliff to his left. He had to take it slow and easy even as the maniac kept popping off shots at him.

As calm as he could, he spoke into his mic, "Don't come down here yet, stay in the trees."

"Damn! Get out of there, Sam! Now!"

Despite the continued barrage of bullets, he chuckled. "Oh, honey, don't you think I'm going as fast as I can?"

"Then move it faster, buster!"

Puffs of snow and rock bounced up from the hillside, spraying Sam and the sled. If only he could take his attention from the trail and free a hand to fire back. Every ounce of concentration needed to be on negotiating the hillside or the bullets wouldn't matter, he'd fall to his death anyway.

Knowing he wouldn't make it if he didn't let the dogs have their heads, he let up on the brake and shouted, "Go! Go! Go!"

Sam said a silent prayer and hung on for dear life. Leaning into the slope, he balanced on one runner to keep the sled from falling over the edge.

He could see the opposite side. The lead dogs arrived first, then the wheel dogs. More bullets winged by, peppering the sled bag and pinging off the sled. Sensing danger, the dogs pulled harder and faster and Sam shouted, urging them on.

Just as the last of the dogs made it to the other side, the sled hit a bump and skittered off the trail, the back end tipping downward. Sam held on with all his strength.

KAT REACHED the top of the drop about the time the bullets started flying. She held her team in check, burying her snow hook in the ground. The team barked and strained in their harnesses, slowing to a reluctant halt.

Loki looked at Kat for direction. He whined and winced with each gunshot.

Kat scanned the uphill slope for the shooter, but there were too many rocks and trees to hide behind. After two very long minutes, she released the foot brake and lifted the snow hook, easing forward. "Sam?"

No response.

Her blood thundered against her ears. "Sam?" Sensing her urgency, the dogs picked up speed until they disappeared around a corner to the right. Kat pounded the foot brake again, forcing the dogs to skid to a halt before crossing the wide-open hillside. Another scan uphill yielded nothing more than the first time. The sniper had quit shooting, but Kat couldn't see whether or not he'd left.

Kat inhaled deeply and let it out. "Let's go!" The dogs leaped forward.

Sam's team clung to the trail on the other side of the

hill. The sled listed to the side several feet below, caught in the branches of a spruce tree. Sam, in his bright red jacket and matching pants, hung like an ornament from the branches, holding tight to keep Hammer from sliding off the top of the sled bag. Three hundred pounds of sled weighed down the frantic team scrambling to pull free.

Her heart pounding against her ribs, Kat knew what she had to do. She couldn't stand by and wait for Sam's sled to break through the branches and crash over the cliffs, carrying Sam and his team with it.

"Let's go!" The dogs strained against their harnesses, building up the speed necessary to get them across the sloped trail. The sled bumped and slid sideways. Kat leaned hard on the right runner, lifting the left runner out of the snow, forcing the weight of the sled to hug the uphill slope. If the sled tipped back, they'd be sliding down the slope so fast, they couldn't recover.

Sweat built beneath the layers of clothing, and the strain of leaning the heavy sled made her arms and legs shake.

"Gee!" She urged her team to the right and a little above where Sam's lead dogs dug into the trail with their claws. With little room to maneuver, she didn't want to cause the huskies to lose their grip and plunge back down the steep slope. When the lead dogs reached the opposite side, Kat didn't pause to breathe a sigh of relief. Not until the entire team and the laden sled were safe did she loosen her death grip on the handlebar.

She pulled ahead of Sam's team and dug her snow hook into the snow. "Whoa!" Kat bounded to the edge of the trail.

"Stay back!" Sam called out, clinging to the branch of the tree. "The snow is slipping away. I don't want you caught in it."

The sled perched on a heavy branch bent nearly double. Hammer clung to the top, whining and staring up at Kat as if pleading with her to save him.

An ominous cracking sound made Kat's eyes widen.

Kat shouted, "Hang on!" Then she ran back to her team, unhooked the carabiner from the sled and hooked her gangline in front of Striker. "Let's go!"

With the combined efforts of thirty-one dogs, the sled moved forward.

"Stand clear!" Sam shouted. The sled pulled free of the branch and crashed to the rear against the slope.

The dogs slid backward in the snow. Kat grabbed Loki's harness and leaned all her weight into pulling them forward. Before long, the team got their feet beneath them, and one by one the dogs worked their way over the edge of the cliff and onto the trail. Finally, the sled runners appeared aimed practically to the sky before dropping with a hard thump onto the snowy trail.

Sam still held on to the back, his hands rooting Hammer in place.

"Whoa!" Kat called out. The dogs stopped, the long line of animals all looking back to her, waiting for further instruction. Although their chests heaved and their heads hung, their tails wagged.

"Good dogs." Kat breathed for the first time in what felt like hours.

"Yes, good dogs." Sam patted Hammer's head and strode to Kat, engulfing her in a fierce hug.

For a moment, Kat clung to his jacket front, her knees shaking. With more treacherous trail still ahead, she couldn't afford to lose it now. Sam had come damn close to being killed by their sniper, they deserved a little cling-time, so Kat held on until the shaking stopped. Tears soon followed, trickling from the corners of her eyes into her goggles. Embarrassed, she leaned back and pulled her goggles over her head. Refusing to look him in the eye, she swiped at the moisture on her cheeks before the cold could freeze it.

"Are those tears?"

"No," she denied, rubbing harder this time with her woolen scarf.

He chuckled, stripping his goggles from his head. "I didn't think the brave Kat Sikes ever shed a tear in public."

"I never do, and I wouldn't call this public." She slapped his chest. "Don't ever scare me like that again!"

"Trust me, I didn't intend to." He tugged his glove off his hand with his teeth. Using the pad of his warm thumb, he brushed a tear across her cheek. "I owe you big-time, Sikes."

"You'd have done the same for me." She should move away from him, but she was afraid if she did, she'd fall flat on her face. Not only had the scare knocked ten years off her life, but it had left her with limp knees. Or was it Sam's thumb touching her skin that sent tremors throughout her body?

Kat made the next mistake of looking up into his

gaze. Eyes the lush green of the Alaskan marshes in the spring stared down at her. If she wasn't careful she could fall into those eyes and drown. She dropped her gaze to avoid his gentle look, only to focus on his lips.

Those same lips had pressed to the tip of her nose last night, she didn't doubt it in the least. Her body hummed with the knowledge, her mouth watering for a taste of them against hers.

His full, sexy lips moved. "You think we should…" His words faded off as if he forgot what he was going to say.

It didn't matter, Kat wasn't listening. Between the giddy relief of Sam's near miss and the headier sensation that she was about to be kissed, her brain quit functioning. "Huh?"

"Oh, hell." His head dropped forward and he claimed her lips. Despite the layers of cold-weather gear, he pulled her to him, his hands circling the back of her neck, drawing her closer.

Kat sank into him, her lips opening to the gentle pressure of his.

His tongue slid across her teeth and darted in to tangle with hers. He tasted of coffee and mint, and the kiss warmed her to the core and lower. For the first time since Marty's death, Kat felt the tug of desire, deep, carnal sensations shocking in their intensity and timing.

Kat gasped and pushed away, her gloved fingers covering her swollen lips. "What are you doing?"

"Something I've wanted to do for a long time." Sam's hands rubbed down the sides of her arms.

She opened her mouth to say she'd been thinking about it, too, but she couldn't, not yet.

A cool wind slapped against her heated skin, reminding her they had the rest of this hill to navigate before they were out of natural danger and line of fire. Not to mention, they had an entire race to complete before they could safely return home. With less care than desperation, she jammed her goggles over her eyes, effectively cutting off any visual display of emotion. "We need to get off this mountain and rest the teams."

For a moment his hand held her in place, and then he dropped his hold, fitting his goggles over his eyes. "You're right. We need to get down the rest of the hill. Our snowmobile guy might have more tricks up his sleeve and I'd just as soon be off this particular playing field before he springs them on us."

CROSSING DOWN the steep hillside, Sam took the lead again. No bullets rang out this time, for which he breathed a sigh. Once again, Kat had proven her abilities and stoic persistence in getting the job done no matter the danger to herself.

When he'd cleared the edge of the cliff and found his team and himself on relatively safe ground, his first thought had been to grab Kat and hold on and never let go again.

For one precious moment, he'd thought Kat felt the same. Then reality returned and he reminded himself, she was a widow. As much as he'd wanted to continue holding her, he didn't have a claim to her heart.

With his arms and shoulders aching, he negotiated the downhill plunge into Happy River Valley, never happier to be on flat, solid ground—or ice, as the case might be.

He stopped in the shelter of some trees and waited for Kat to pull in alongside. She stepped from the runners of her sled and flexed her wrists. The dogs plopped to the ground, as if they too were relieved to make the descent in one piece.

Sam pulled out a hunk of beef jerky and handed a piece to Kat. "I've been thinking."

She took it, pushing her scarf down to take a bite. "Should I be worried?"

"Maybe." He stared back the way they'd come. "After what happened on that hill, I'm going to pull out of the race at the next checkpoint."

Kat's mouth stopped in midchew and her cheeks lost most of their rosy hue. "Pull out?"

Sam faced her and nodded. "I can't continue, knowing someone will be there to sabotage me every step of the way and maybe take out another contestant besides me."

"You're letting someone else call the shots for you? What if that's what he wants? What if he wants someone else to win at all costs?" The words she spoke echoed through the earphone in his left ear.

"That's a chance I'll take. What if you'd been right behind me on that hillside during all that gunfire?"

"What if I had?" She shrugged, although her movement turned into a shiver. "We'd have managed."

Sam caught the movement. She'd been scared just as badly as he had. "No, you could have been killed."

"But I wasn't." Her lips thinned.

"What if someone else had been behind me? The fact someone is after me puts everyone else in danger. I'm pulling out."

"No, you're not." The voice in Sam's ear was lower than Kat's and her lips hadn't moved.

Kat's eyes widened. "Who's on this frequency?"

"That's for me to know and you to figure out," a voice said. He sounded as if he spoke through a glove, his deep voice muffled and unrecognizable.

"Who are you, and what do you want?" Sam spoke slowly and clearly into the lip mic, his gaze panning the canyon walls and surrounding hills.

"Let's just say, I have an interest in seeing you suffer."

"Who? Sam?" Kat asked.

"Yeah, Sam, or whatever he's calling himself today."

Sam shot her a fierce look and made a slicing motion over his throat. He didn't want this guy to target Kat, as well. "If it's me you want, come and get me."

Kat's eyes widened behind the protective shield of her goggles and she shook her head violently.

"All in good time." The voice paused. "Know this. If either you or your girlfriend drop from this race, I'll kill a contestant every time the clock strikes twelve. And just to show you how much I mean it, the clock just struck twelve." The sound of an engine revved in Sam's earphone. "You'll find your proof at the bottom of Happy River Canyon just past Long Lake."

Then silence.

Kat set her radio to mute and she nodded at Sam for him to do the same. While they could hear their tormentor, he couldn't hear them.

"Do you think he's killed someone?" Kat whipped off her goggles, her eyes wild, her face pale.

Sam's lips pressed together, a knot forming in his gut.

"Oh God." Kat's eyes squeezed shut and her head dropped low for a few seconds. The next moment, she settled her goggles in place, adjusted her scarf over her mouth and shouted, "Let's go!"

Sam followed her out of Happy River Canyon, reflecting on the irony of where they were and what was occurring. The ravine leading up Happy River Hill was slowgoing and strenuous. Half the time, he and Kat jogged up the hill behind their sleds to ease the burden on the team. A heavy weight rested on Sam's chest, squeezing the breath right out of him. Had the madman targeted an innocent just to prove a point?

What had Sam done so monumentally heinous to inspire a hatred so great? He'd known people to kill over oil rights and politics, but those instances were few and far between. Could this be one of them?

Now that he knew his conversations with Kat had been monitored, he didn't feel comfortable talking over the radio. He kept his mic on mute. If he got in a tight situation, he would switch it back on.

Still on one of the most dangerous legs of the race, Sam didn't push too fast. He could only take the team to their limits, not beyond, or he and his dogs would be dead at the bottom of some canyon. Several times along the trail, his runners had skidded sideways on treacherous hillsides, but he maintained his speed and kept the dogs moving past the bad spots.

Where he could slow and wait, he did to ensure Kat made it through, as well.

When he passed Long Lake and began the steep descent to the ridge running along the south side of Happy River Valley, he heard dogs baying ahead. His own team barked and howled in response. The trail crossed a hillside where the right side dropped off a hundred feet into Happy River Canyon. With all the skill and conviction he could muster, Sam fought to control the dogs over the roots, rocks and uneven trail conditions. Halfway across, Sam noticed a part of the trail had been chiseled away from the hillside. The dogs managed the spot fine, and by leaning his sled onto one runner, Sam did, too.

The howling increased and Sam risked a glance to the bottom of the drop-off.

"Damn." An icy hand gripped his gut. Somehow, he'd hoped his tormentor hadn't followed through on his threat. Sam had hoped he'd find a musher if not well and resting, at least only wounded and salvageable if they got to him in time.

From the looks of things, this musher had reached the end of this particular race.

Sam maintained his course until they had completely traversed the dangerous hillside, then he stomped his foot brake. "Whoa!" Even before the sled came to a complete halt, he leaped from the runners and ran back to the drop-off, switching his mic from mute to on. He could hear Kat's team howling around the corner. "Don't start across the hillside yet. Stop short."

"Why?"

"We have a musher at the bottom of the canyon. I'm going down."

The sled had crashed into a dozen pieces, supplies scattered across the rocks. A man wearing a black and royal-blue parka lay spread-eagle, his goggles lying a yard away.

Sam recognized him as one of the men who'd left the camp early that morning after the visit from the moose.

Picking his way down the side of the hill, Sam eventually made it to the canyon floor, where he peeled off his gloves and felt for a pulse.

Some of the dogs in the canyon whined and struggled against their tangled necklines, while others remained lifeless beneath the weight of the sled.

The man lay on his back with his eyes closed and his face a deathly white.

When he felt the faint pulse, Sam breathed a sigh. Even though the fall hadn't killed him when his head struck a large boulder, getting him out of the canyon and on to the next checkpoint might.

Kat half climbed, half slid down the hill to where Sam knelt in the snow.

"It's George Engle." She shoved a fist against her mouth and staggered to her feet. There she hunched over, her shoulders heaving.

Sam stood and held her shoulders as Kat tossed what little contents remained in her stomach. When she straightened he handed her a tissue from one of his pockets. "Here."

Her eyes watered and her face was a sallow shade of pale green. "Thanks. I don't know what's the matter with me. It's not like I haven't seen a dead man before and George isn't even dead."

Sam didn't say "yet." If they didn't get him out of the cold and back to a hospital, he might end up that way.

Sam stared into Kat's eyes as he switched his mic on. "Okay, you made your point. We'll stay in the race."

"Good, because I have so much more planned for you." The low voice sounded all too smug. "And don't get any ideas about calling in the feds or it'll just get worse on the other mushers."

"Bastard."

"Tsk, tsk. Temper."

Sam muted his mic and stared across the snow at Kat. "We have to find him before he hurts someone else."

"How? All we have are teams of dogs. He's got a high-speed snowmobile and a high-powered rifle."

"Maybe it's time to call in some of your government pals."

Kat's brow furrowed. "You heard him, no feds."

"This guy plays by his own rules, it's about time we play by a few of our own."

HANDS SHAKING, Kat punched in the code on her satellite phone.

"Hey, girl," Tazer answered. "Did you know your brother cheats at Monopoly?"

Paul's voice sounded in the earpiece. "Do not. I can't help it if she's a sore loser."

Her chest constricted. By the sound of it, everything was normal back home. Kat wished she were there now, instead of staring down at the chilling reminder she and Sam were now in a race for their lives. "Tazer, I need to speak with Royce."

"Sure. But we just found out Al's not the only one counting on Sam finding marketable oil. James Blalock just spoke in Congress about opening more Alaskan land to oil exploration and he's telling them the oil Sam found is worth going after."

"It is, is it?" Kat stared into Sam's eyes. "Does he have enough at stake to want Sam dead?"

"He owns a lot of the land in the proposed area. My guess is he wants the approval to drill for oil so that he can profit from either the sale of the land or the mineral rights."

"So let me get this straight. Al Fendley needs the roads to improve business and pay off debt, and Senator Blalock wants to profit off the sale of land or mineral rights?" She spoke clearly and directed her conclusions at Sam as much as at Tazer.

Sam's lips pressed into a thin line.

"That sums it up," Tazer responded.

"Get me Royce. We've had a few challenges of our own."

"Ah, geez." Tazer sighed. "That guy shoot at you again?"

"Yeah."

"Did you or Sam get hurt?"

"No, thank goodness. He attacked one of the other mushers in the race."

"Not good."

Kat almost laughed at her understatement. She might have if an innocent man wasn't growing cold on the ground as they stood around talking. She wondered if he had a family waiting for him back home.

"Then he's not just after Sam?" Tazer's voice broke through Kat's morose thoughts.

"Yes, he is. He did it to prove he would kill more mushers if Sam or I dropped out of the race before reaching Nome."

"Holy mother." Tazer's voice dropped to a flat hard tone. "I'm on it."

Chapter Eight

Darkness cloaked the countryside around the small settlement of Rainy Pass. Sam had never been so glad to see the icy runway on Puntilla Lake and the lights of the log buildings of Rainy Pass Lodge.

Despite how late it was, people streamed out of the lodge to greet them. He and Kat had sent George's team ahead with a note attached to the lead dog's harness. It had taken them almost an hour to pull George out of the canyon and load him on Sam's sled. With the help of their dogs, they managed to get him out of there with minimal additional injury.

Apparently George's team had arrived. Before Sam's sled slid to a halt, they were hammered with questions.

Sam unzipped his sled bag and flipped it back, revealing George's limp body wrapped in sleeping bags.

"Is he dead?" one of the mushers asked.

"No." Sam stepped back so that the checkpoint volunteers could lift George from his resting place. "He's been unconscious since we found him. Best thing would be to get him warm and then to a hospital as soon as possible."

Kat's sled pulled up beside Sam's. She stepped off the runners and crossed to stand beside him, holding out her hand to clasp his gloved one.

A racing official stepped forward. "What happened?"

"He fell into Happy River Canyon this side of Long Lake." Sam left off the part where a snowmobile had run George off the hillside and that the tracks indicated the machine had clipped the sled, ensuring it would take the one-hundred-foot fall. Sam also skipped the part about the terrorist really being after him and that he would kill more contestants if Sam didn't continue the race.

If he could, Sam would have the entire Iditarod called off immediately. But too many mushers were scattered through the hills to bring them all in. Others would end up dead before they could collect everyone.

Kat squeezed his hand through the glove as if she sensed his frustration. He hated that she was involved in this race to the death. At the same time, her presence infused a little sanity and balance to a no-win situation. If she was an S.O.S. agent, she had to be fearless, resourceful and ready for anything. If he had to have anyone by his side through this ordeal, she'd be his first choice.

The checkpoint officials and some of the other mushers lifted George from Sam's sled and carried him to one of the buildings. They'd notify George's family and transport him back to Anchorage. Sam and Kat couldn't do any more for him than they already had.

The veterinarian inspected the two teams and promised to have Hammer flown to Anchorage, as well, where he'd be cared for by prisoners until Sam could collect him after the race.

If Sam survived. Based on the turn of events, he'd began to have doubts. His fists tightened. He'd be damned if he let this guy take him or Kat down.

Sam fed the dogs and gave them fresh straw to bed down in. Then he stared at the lodge with the bright yellow lights glowing from the windows. After being out on the trail, the thought of going back into a civilized building didn't fit, but his body demanded a real meal and a place to clean up.

Carrying her sleeping bag and a small bag of toiletries, Kat tromped through the snow toward him. "Think we can find a place inside to catch a few hours' sleep?" Her shoulders were slumped and she was dragging. With only about four hours' sleep in the past forty-eight, she had to be ready to drop.

"I think so. But first we need to eat."

"I'm not as hungry as I am tired."

"Maybe so, but you need to eat. We should be ready for anything."

HANDS AND LEGS aching from the grueling trek through the passes, Kat could barely keep her head up to eat the tasty stew. But the warm chunks of beef and potatoes slid down her throat, increasing her lethargy until she set her spoon aside and lay back in her sleeping bag. "Wake me up at midnight. We need to be at the summit of Rainy Pass by dawn…" The last of her words faded off as her eyelids closed and she drifted into a troubled sleep.

She had just left Wasilla where she'd begun the first leg of the Iditarod. Her team trotted out in front of her, all sixteen dogs happy, healthy and ready to run in the sunshine bouncing off the glaringly white, snow-covered trail.

The more the dogs ran, the darker the sky grew. Ahead, another musher stayed just within sight. Kat couldn't make out his parka color but, deep inside, she was sure it was someone she cared about, someone she loved. Was it Marty?

Was Marty ahead of her on the trail? Had the explosion in Dindi all been an elaborate hoax to make someone think he'd died and he hadn't?

"Let's go!" she yelled to her team, urging them faster.

The trail led up a twisted ravine and through a heavily wooded area. For a long time she couldn't see the musher.

Her heart thundered against her chest, her hands sweating inside her gloves. Just as she knew this person was someone she cared about, she knew something bad was about to happen.

She climbed the trail to the top of a ridge and one by one her dogs disappeared as if they'd fallen off the end of the earth. When she reached the top, the sled balanced on the edge before the front end tipped forward.

She swallowed the scream rising in her throat. Her team was running as fast as they could down a steep slope. Kat jammed her foot on the brake, pressing it into the snow as hard as she could. Even throwing out her snow hook didn't slow the sled. The trail rounded a curve and she leaned as hard as she could on the inside runner to keep the sled from tipping over.

Her dogs stopped on the other side of the curve, her sled slowing to a standstill. When she looked out across the trail, she could see the musher crossing the side of a hill. A heavy rumbling sound shook the earth. As she watched, a wall of snow lifted the musher, sled and dogs and carried them away in a billowy cloud of dirty white.

With her breath trapped in her throat, Kat held on to her handlebar. As dust, snow and debris settled, she inched her way to the bottom of a canyon. No sign of the musher, his sled or dogs could be seen. Desperate to find him, she clawed at the snow, digging away layer after layer until she reached the fur-lined hood of a parka. Scraping snow and ice away from his face, she stared down into the lifeless face of her husband.

But he was already dead. He'd died over a year ago.

She staggered to her feet and backed away until she hit a wall. Only, the wall moved, wrapping around her.

Kat struggled as it trapped her arms against her sides. Then her captor turned her to face him and she looked up into Sam's eyes. "Let him go, Kat. Marty's dead. Let him go."

She stared up into Sam's face. When she looked back toward Marty, his face disappeared and in its place was that of George Engle's. George was in the fall, not Marty, because Marty died over a year ago.

Tears welled in her eyes and choked the air from her

throat. Darkness enveloped her, sucking her down into a pit. Marty had died and left her alone. Tremors started in her hands working their way up her arms and into her body until every part of her shook.

"It's okay, Kat." Sam's voice broke through her grief and pulled her up from the dark well of despair into the light. "I've got you covered, Kat. You'll be okay."

Kat nestled against Sam's neck, letting him hold her close until her body stopped trembling and her tears dried. All the while the thought echoed in her head, "Marty died, let him go."

"HEY, MUCH AS I LIKE holding you, it's midnight." Sam's breath stirred the loose tendrils of her hair on her right cheek. As sleep faded and awareness set root, Kat realized she was tucked against Sam, spoon-style, her bottom and back against his torso and hips.

She sat upright, her cheeks burning. "I'm sorry. Here I was hogging the floor." She leaped to her feet and quickly rolled her sleeping bag, refusing to look into Sam's face. How long had she been lying against him?

Her blood hummed with the possibilities. Not that they had done anything. Not with a roomful of mushers, some sleeping, some just getting up and some settling in for a nap around the potbellied, wood-burning stove.

Kat snatched her boots from in front of the stove and shoved her feet into their warm interior. If they hurried they could be back on the trail in less than fifteen minutes. Kat dared a look at Sam.

He didn't make the situation worse by grinning. He

acted as if holding her through the night was the most natural thing. Perhaps as natural as lying on a floor in a remote cabin with a variety of men and women set on completing a grueling race.

Willing her heart to settle into a normal rhythm, Kat inhaled and exhaled several times before hefting her bag. Someone had coffee brewing, the rich aroma filling the confines of the cabin and making her mouth water. She hoped it was open to anyone who wanted some, because right now she needed a jolt of caffeine to bring her fully awake and back to her senses.

Kat filled her canteen cup with the fresh coffee and headed for the door, the walls of the small checkpoint cabin closing in around her. On the one hand, she felt safe from the maniac while inside the solid log walls. On the other, she needed to escape into the wide-open countryside. Her dream still lingered, leaving her shaken and less rested than she should be after four hours' sleep. With the beginnings of an attack of claustrophobia coming on, Kat threaded her way over the bodies lying around the stove and shoved her way out the door.

"Are you okay?" Sam closed the door behind him and hooked an arm around Kat's waist as if it belonged there.

When all she wanted to do was lean back and let him shoulder the entire burden, Kat moved out of reach. "I'm fine. Why?"

"You didn't sleep well, and you ran out of the cabin as if your tail was on fire. What gives?"

Kat threw her empty hand in the air and laughed.

"What's wrong? We have a nutcase after you, a man nearly dies and we still have nine hundred miles left in this race. You tell me, what's wrong with this picture?"

Sam turned her. "You were dreaming of Marty, weren't you?"

"How did you know?" Now was not a good time for tears to well in her eyes. She stared down into her canteen cup full of coffee as if it held all the answers.

"I heard you say his name while you slept." He grabbed both of her shoulders, careful not to spill her coffee.

"Well, you had no right to eavesdrop on my dream." Her tears bubbled over and streamed down her cheeks, the moisture stinging in the frigid night air. She wouldn't tell him he'd been in her dream, too.

"It's hard to lose someone you love. I know. It hurts." He brushed a tear from her cheek. "Eventually the pain fades, but you never forget."

"Never?"

"Do you really want to?"

Kat stared into his eyes, reflecting the light from the window. "No." She'd loved Marty, and she didn't want to forget any of the time they'd had together.

"Then don't let him go. But don't stop living, either."

Kat hadn't realized how lonely she'd been before Marty came along. Since his death, she had been ten times more afraid to have another relationship. She couldn't handle the pain of loss all over again.

Looking into Sam's face, she knew what kind of man he was. The kind who took care of his own, who loved fiercely and expected the same in return. The kind of man she could fall in love with very easily. A man she could be falling for already.

Her hand shook, the coffee in the canteen cup sloshing over the edge, burning her fingers. "Ouch!"

Sam reached for her hands. "You should be more careful."

"You're telling me?" She forced laughter she didn't feel and moved back another step until he let go. She drank one more scalding swallow, the hot liquid sizzling a path down her esophagus to her belly.

The satellite phone in Kat's pocket vibrated, giving her the perfect excuse to put even more distance between herself and Sam. Although the state of Alaska wouldn't be enough distance at the moment.

She tromped through the snow toward the lake, away from the prying eyes of officials.

Sam followed.

Once out of sight of the cabins, she pushed aside her parka hood and pressed the phone to her ear. "Kat here."

"This is Royce, let me talk to Sam."

SAM WALKED farther away from the cabin, heading toward Puntilla Lake. He didn't want those inside resting or those outside caring for their animals to overhear his conversation. "Hi, Royce. It's been a long time."

"Too long. It's good to hear from you, Sam."

"Same." And it was. Royce had been his friend before things went wrong on the job and Sam liked to think he still was.

"I understand things aren't going so well up there. Wanna give me the scoop?"

"Someone's got it in for me and he's determined to stretch the punishment along the length of the Iditarod."

"Sadistic bastard."

"You're telling me." Sam stared across the moonlit frozen lake. "He knows what makes me mad and he's pushing all my buttons."

"You okay? Has he hurt you?"

"He got in some target practice earlier, but we made it through unscathed. Although George Engle didn't."

"He the guy you two found at the bottom of the canyon?"

"Yeah. He's alive, but I'm not sure he'll make it." Anger surged through him, and Sam wanted to lash out, punch someone and kill this maniac for what he was doing. "George has a wife and two kids back in Big Lake. He doesn't deserve this."

Royce paused. "Okay, what do you want me to do? I can send more people. I can fly Tazer into one of the checkpoints within the hour. You're on the inside, tell me what will help most."

"More than anything, I need to know who I'm dealing with and why he's after me." A frigid breeze blew across the frozen lake, biting at Sam's exposed fingers. He pulled his gloves from his pocket and slipped them on, balancing the phone between his chin and shoulder. "He's good with a gun and he has access to Kat's radio frequency."

"Practically every man in Alaska is good with a gun,"

Royce reasoned. "And anyone with a little techno savvy can tap into open frequencies."

"I know Tazer's been digging into the backgrounds of the race participants, but who else? Can you put your ear to the ground in Washington and find out if Senator Blalock has a contract out on me over this oil deal? I'm grasping at straws. I don't want anyone else hurt because of me."

"I'll do that, and I'll send Tazer out to the next checkpoint that has a runway and fly Casanova Valdez and Sean McNeal out to Washington within the next hour. And Sam?"

Talking with Royce was like old times. Better times. Times before he'd botched the mission in Saudi and a little girl died for it. He missed his affiliation with the S.O.S. More than he'd realized. "Yes, sir?"

"You can't take it so personally." Royce's voice was deep, insistent, as convincing as he could be over a static-filled satellite phone. "You aren't hurting these people. Some jerk is out there doing this."

"I won't have anyone else die because of my actions."

"Is this about the folks on the Iditarod or is it really about Saudi?" Royce asked.

The punch to his gut answered that question. Sam didn't dignify Royce's question with a response. "Just find out about Blalock and send in the cavalry."

"Will do."

Sam hit the Off button, the urge to throw the satellite phone across the frozen lake strong.

A gloved hand pressed against his shoulder. "You

okay?" Kat moved up beside him and relieved him of the phone, stuffing it into her pocket.

"Yeah, I'm fine." George Engle was on his way to a hospital in Anchorage, but Sam was so damn fine, he could crush rocks with his teeth. "Didn't you say we need to make the summit by dawn?"

"Yes." She lifted a bucket. "Just coming for water to get started feeding the gang." When she moved toward the hole drilled through the ice in the lake, Sam's hand stopped her.

"I'm sorry you've been dragged into this."

She stared at him, her bright blue eyes reflecting the moonlight. Soft tendrils of her midnight-black hair floated about her cheek. "I'm not. I needed a challenge to snap me out of my funk."

Sam shook his head. "That's what I like about you, Sikes."

Her eyes narrowed. "What's that?"

"You're up for the challenge. Not many men or women dare the hardships of the Iditarod, but here you are. And if that's not enough, you're game for a little cat and mouse with a killer." Anger flared. "You're tough, Kat. But I don't want you hurt."

"I can take care of myself."

"You don't understand. This maniac is playing with me. He knows that by hurting others, he'll get to me, damn it. And since you're the closest one to me, he'll hurt you to hurt me."

"Sam, I can take care of myself," she repeated as if

to a not-so-bright child. Kat's clear blue eyes flashed in the moonlight and her chin jutted out.

Her confidence and courage filled his chest with a warmth he hadn't felt in years. At the same time it made him all the angrier at his faceless assassin. As he stared down at Kat, his body relived the feeling of hers pressed against him in her sleep. Longing swelled into a deep ache.

He knew he was wrong to do it, and he'd regret it later, but he did it anyway. Sam's hands settled on her shoulders. "I know you can take care of yourself. But for some strange reason, I want to take care of you. Must be something in your eyes."

For a long moment he stared into those eyes glistening like glacier ice, catching the stars overhead. Then he pulled her against him, his lips pressing down hard over hers. Anger, passion, frustration all welled inside him and poured into his kiss.

Kat's eyes widened, her mouth responding to the pressure of his, softening and opening to the thrust of his tongue.

Locked in a kiss that shouldn't have happened, Sam couldn't stop what he'd started and Kat didn't seem inclined to break it off, either. His fingers dug into her thick black hair, circling behind her neck to hold her close. That ache in his belly moved farther south, swelling and straining against his button-fly jeans. He moved closer, the bulk of their winter garb blocking more intimate contact.

A cold wind slipped across the lake, stirring up a dusting of powdery snow and chilling Sam's cheeks and the tip of his nose. The bite of the breeze brought him back to earth, reminding him he was still in Alaska standing out in the snow when they should be moving on to the summit.

Sam broke away, his arms falling to his sides.

For a moment, Kat stood still, eyes glazed, her lips parted, steam blowing gently between them.

Before she could lodge her protest, he snagged the bucket from where she'd dropped it in the snow. He carried it to the hole in the ice, thinking only a dip in the frozen lake could cool his raging passion at this point.

Fool! He shouldn't have started something he couldn't finish. With the bottom of the bucket, he banged against the thin film of ice already forming over the hole. When it broke through, he dipped the bucket in, careful not to soak his gloved hand.

Why had he kissed her? If his pursuer saw him, he'd certainly know Kat was the key to bringing him down. Hurt Kat, and he'd hurt Sam. His gaze panned the lake and surrounding hills as if he could see into the shadows. Nothing stirred in the cold night air. Nothing but the wind and a low layer of blowing snow.

When he returned to Kat's side, her face was set in an unreadable mask.

A small part of Sam was disappointed and yet relieved. He didn't want the kiss to make a difference in their working relationship.

But it did. Much as he wanted to deny it, he'd enjoyed holding her close last night when she'd cried out in her sleep. Not only had she cried out Marty's name, she'd called out his name, as well, seeking comfort in *his* arms.

AFTER FEEDING and watering the dogs and tying fresh booties on their feet, Kat tucked her scarf in place and pulled her goggles over her eyes. "Ready?"

Sam nodded at her from behind his sled. "I'll take the lead."

Her team danced around, yelping at being left behind. When Sam had a sufficient lead, she pulled her snow hook from the packed snow and lifted her foot off the brake.

The dogs shot out of the checkpoint. She didn't have to shout, the spirit of competition and their love of running had them straining against their harnesses to catch the lead sled.

Just past midnight, the moon shone bright overhead, reflecting off the white snow, making the night almost as bright as day. They'd make the summit of Rainy Pass by dawn, easily.

If they didn't run into more trouble from their mystery creep.

A chill snaked down Kat's spine. The vision of George Engle lying at the bottom of the canyon, his sled a wreck and several of his dogs dead, played like a rerun over and over in her head.

The teams climbed out of the valley into the tree line. At first, every shadow made Kat jump. At this rate, the stress would wear her out before she made it to the next checkpoint. She relaxed, remaining alert but refusing to be a nervous wreck.

The trail led down a steep ravine and back up until the team emerged onto the open tundra. Sheltered in the trees, she hadn't realized how much the wind had picked up.

Out in the open, with nothing to stop or slow the arctic winds, she was hit by the force. Although there hadn't been a cloud in the sky, Kat couldn't see the team in front of her. The wind blew the snow low and hard, creating a ground blizzard. She could see fine above the dogs, but not through the low-blowing snow. The normal four-foot-high fluorescent orange trail markers were completely obliterated. Instead she watched for the six-foot-high wooden tripods placed every few hundred yards for just this kind of weather.

Other than making her legs ache from leaning against the wind for a couple of hours, she crossed the tundra unscathed. No one fired at her while she was in the open. Reassured by the view she had of Sam's head and shoulders above the blowing snow in the distance, she kept moving.

The dogs ran strong and steady, neither slowing nor requiring a rest stop.

After ten miles on the tundra, Kat greeted the entrance to Rainy Pass with a combination of relief and dread. Besides the natural hazards, what man-created hazard would be lurking in the trees or behind the clumps of willow bushes?

"Watch for overflow as you approach the river," Sam said into her ear. "It's very slick and rough."

Although they'd changed frequencies on the radio before they left Rainy Pass Lodge, they hadn't spoken in several hours, extremely aware of their eavesdropper. Kat missed talking to him as they traversed the trail; it passed the time and made the trip seem shorter. "Are you okay?"

"Slid sideways a couple times, but doing fine." His words were short, not inviting further conversation.

Nor did Kat want to give their pursuer the opportunity to tune in again to their frequency. Maintaining radio silence was the best way to keep him off.

When Kat hit the overflow, she thought she was ready, but her sled bounced and skidded sideways, taking the dogs with it. She slammed against another bump, the sled creaking but remaining in one piece.

The dogs' feet slipped and they struggled to gain purchase to maintain forward momentum. Kat pedaled with one foot on the ice and one on the runner. She knew better than to get off the sled, she'd be flat on her backside in a moment.

Between her pedaling and the dogs scrambling, they finally made it onto snow again, where they picked up speed. Soon they were weaving through clumps of bushes and bumping over buffalo grass in the frozen creek, making basketball-size bumps in the ice. The trail steadily climbed, with occasional side-hill areas where snow was minimal, making it harder for the sled to traverse.

At one point the dogs spotted caribou near the sides of the valley. In their excitement, they leaped forward, racing past Rainy Pass Lake and on to the summit. At the top of the hill leading down into Pass Fork Valley, Kat stomped her foot brake. She barely had time to think about Sam and the danger lurking in the shadows. If she wanted to remain in one piece, she had to focus all her attention on the trail.

Into the timberline, the path twisted around rocky ravines, following a creek. Kat scanned the area immediately in front of the sled, on the alert for holes in the ice.

Another bright yellow highway sign warned her to Watch Your Ass, marking the entrance to Dalzell Gorge. Kat leaned hard on her foot brake. "Whoa!"

The dogs disappeared over the edge of the hill and the sled followed in the two-hundred-foot descent into Dalzell Gorge. Kat had been here before, when the conditions were favorable, but she'd heard nightmarish tales of the trouble mushers experienced in the gorge.

The sun glinted off the ice and running water below. Kat groaned and took a deep breath before hastily crossing back and forth across the creek on snow bridges, tipping the sled onto one runner when she risked falling into open water. A couple times, her momentum slid her across the ice, heading toward open water, but the dogs kept pulling her forward and out of danger.

When her team and sled finally emerged from Dalzell Gorge, Kat breathed a sigh of relief. Sam's team was far ahead on the Tatina River.

Her relief lasted all of two seconds when her runners hit glare ice and the sled skidded sideways. The left runner bounced against a chunk of overflow ice and the entire sled tipped. Kat fought to keep it upright, but it fell on its side, taking her with it.

Kat's shoulder, then her hip, hit the hard surface. While pain radiated through her, she didn't let go of the handlebar. The dogs, bound and determined to catch the team in front of them, raced on, dragging her and the fallen sled along the rough river surface.

Every time Kat tried to get her feet beneath her, she hit a patch of ice and slammed down again. Unable to see what was coming, she held on, her body taking the beating of a lifetime, bouncing over every rough patch of overflow.

Several times she shouted, "Whoa!," but each time she hit a bump that knocked the air from her, making her call sound more like a weak cough.

When Kat thought she couldn't hang on any longer, the dogs pulled the sled up onto the riverbank and she was able to scramble to her feet. "Whoa!"

With the sled lying on a bit of a slope, she didn't have far to go to push it upright and back on its runners. Bruised and shaken, she climbed onto the skids and called out, "Let's go!" She couldn't see Sam any longer and she didn't like being separated from him for any length of time.

What if something happened to him?

No longer worried about her own predicament, Kat sagged against the handlebar as the sled continued its brutally bumpy ride along the trail. Shouting encouragement, she urged the dogs to hurry. How long had Sam been out of sight?

The beauty of the Alaska Range was lost on Kat when all she wanted to see was the black and red of Sam's parka in front of her.

Chapter Nine

"Kat?" Sam called into the mic for the tenth time since he'd looked back and couldn't see her or her team following closely behind.

He'd centered his concentration on getting over the rough patches and glare ice on the Tatina River. Now she wasn't responding and he'd moved into the trees, out of sight of the river.

Just short of a mile from the Rohn checkpoint, Sam stomped his foot brake and shouted to the dogs, "Whoa!" He dropped the snow hook in the ground, bringing the sled to a complete stop.

"Kat." He tapped the mic. His pulse quickened until his heart thundered in his chest. Where was she? On a narrow trail, he couldn't easily turn his team around and go look for her. But he would if she didn't show up in the next five minutes.

"Kat!" *Please respond.*

Instead of Kat's sweet tones, the voice he'd come to dread sounded in his ear. "What's the matter, lose your girlfriend?"

Sam swore. "What do you want now?"

"To make your life as miserable as you've made mine." His tone was flat, the undercurrent pure evil.

"What is it I've done to you?"

"Oh, come now. Surely *Sam Russell,* the geological engineer who graduated top of his class at Stanford, is much smarter than that." He paused. "Figure it out."

The dogs stared back at him, awaiting his next command. Sam stepped off the sled and looked behind him, refusing to respond to the man taunting him, worry eating an ulcer into his gut. Where was Kat?

"In the meantime, I've been busy and have a few surprises planned for you. I suggest you and your girlfriend pick up the pace. I wouldn't want you to miss the show, or the show to miss you. Nothing like a game of life-and-death."

A lead weight dropped into the pit of Sam's belly. What the hell did that mean? Had the maniac attacked another musher? Forced to stay on the trail with nothing faster than a team of dogs, Sam couldn't go chasing off after a man on a snowmobile.

"You should make the Rohn checkpoint in the next fifteen minutes. Don't stay long. Once you leave Rohn, I'll let you know more about my surprises. Ah, I see your girlfriend has almost caught up to you. Good."

Sam hit the Mute button.

Dogs barked around a bend in the trail and soon Loki sprang into view, followed by the rest of the team and finally Kat. Her sled had a layer of crusty snow clinging to one side and so did her parka.

When she slid up beside him, he crossed the distance to her. "Why the hell didn't you answer me?"

Kat's brows rose. "Did you try to reach me over the radio?" She removed a glove and dug in her pocket for her receiver. "I had some difficulties on the Tatina River back there. I hope this darn thing isn't broken." After flipping the On/Off button and checking her earpiece, she looked up. "Try it again."

Sam spoke into his mic. "Kat."

A smile lifted the corners of her mouth. "Thank goodness, it still works. That's the side I fell on."

"You fell?" His gaze ran the length of her. "Are you all right?"

"Got crossways on the glare ice and my sled dumped over on its side. I went down with it and the dogs kept going." She gave him a crooked smile. "Nothing feels better than being dragged behind your sled over rough ice."

"Nothing damaged? No concussion?" He tipped her head back and stared into her eyes.

"No, I'm fine, just a little headache."

His hands dropped to his sides. "We're about to have more of a headache."

Her smile slipped downward. "Why?"

"While you were out of touch, our terrorist let me know he's got more planned."

"Crud." She slid the radio back in her pocket. "What next?"

"He said we had to hurry through the Rohn checkpoint, alluding to leaving more surprises farther down the trail."

Her gaze reached through the trees as if searching for the right answer. "We have to stop this race."

"And if we do, he kills an innocent." Sam shook his head.

"How soon did Royce say he could get someone out here?"

"Tazer will be at Nikolai soon. Valdez and McNeal should arrive in Anchorage by nightfall." He hoped that would be soon enough and that they'd be on time. Sam nodded to her sled. "We'd better get going. If someone is in trouble, they won't last long in this cold."

Sam let her take the lead. He liked it better when Kat and her team were ahead of him, where he could keep his eye on them. His heart continued to race in his chest. She was quickly becoming a fixture in his life on the Iditarod Trail.

Her courage and chutzpah, wrapped in a beautiful package, made her all the more appealing. If she weren't such a blatant reminder of his past at the S.O.S., he might like having her around on a more permanent basis.

Although the instinct to protect Kat was strong, Sam knew Kat could take care of herself. It was the rest of the unsuspecting participants, spectators and racing officials he worried about.

KAT PULLED INTO Rohn, anxious to hurry past the checkpoint officials and get on with the race. If someone needed their help, they didn't have time for the formalities of the race checkpoint. But to keep suspicion to a minimum, they had to play the game by the rules.

As she slid to a stop, another sled was departing. The bright yellow parka was like a flag waving saying Al Fendley had just left.

Were they the ones sabotaging Sam? Did they want to win the race that badly? And was a relative rookie a threat to them?

"Was that Al Fendley and his team?" Kat asked the veterinarian, already knowing the answer but hoping for more than just what she'd asked.

She wasn't disappointed. The vet shook his head, staring off at the disappearing Fendley. "Yup. He wasn't too happy when I told him he had to drop two dogs from his team."

"Injuries?"

"One had a cut paw from losing a bootie and the other had a sore shoulder." The vet's attention switched to Kat's team. "Nope, he wasn't too happy dropping down to fourteen. Went off pretty mad."

No, Kat couldn't imagine Al being happy about that, not the way he liked to win. But surely he understood the dogs' health had to come first if he ever hoped to race them again.

While the vet checked each animal, Kat made her own pass, checking and replacing damaged or missing booties and giving each dog a snack. Chowderhead seemed to be favoring his right leg. Rather than risk further injury, she agreed with the vet to remove him from her team and hand him off to the checkpoint officials for transport back to Anchorage. She could still make good time with the fifteen-dog team, but she'd have to keep a close eye on them for injury as their adventure continued.

After the vet left her to check on Sam's team, the satellite phone vibrated in her pocket and Kat scrambled around a building to answer out of sight of the officials.

"Hey, Kat, it's Tazer."

"Where are you?"

"Just arrived in Nikolai. Where are you?"

"Rohn checkpoint. About to head out in the next five minutes." She hoped.

"I've arranged to pick up a snowmobile here and should be on the trail in about half an hour."

Kat shook her head even though Tazer couldn't see her. "I know you can handle a snowmobile, Tazer, but the trail between here and Nikolai is some of the worst in the race. If you aren't familiar, you might get lost or injured."

"I understand and I've been read the riot act by no less then five Alaskan natives. You wouldn't believe the deposit I had to put down just to rent the machine."

"We think we might have trouble somewhere between here and Nikolai and we're not sure what or where along the trail. Our bad guy just said he's got more in store for us, and if we didn't hurry, someone could die."

"Great."

"Tell you what, Tazer, you might be better off staying in Nikolai and nosing around. Our BG might show up there to refuel his snowmobile. Heck, he might be there now."

"Good idea. I'll check around and see if I can learn anything. BG, huh?"

"Yeah, since we don't know who he is, it's shorter than that maniac psycho-killer."

Tazer chuckled. "You have a point."

"We should be in Nikolai tomorrow afternoon, if all hell doesn't break loose on the trail."

"If I don't find anything here by morning, I'll meet you along the trail."

"Be careful. I know you've done missions in extreme climates, but the Alaska Range can be unforgiving at best. Sometimes a sled team can make it through better than a snowmobile."

"Thanks for the warning, sweetie. I'll keep in touch."

Kat stuffed the phone in her pocket and looked around for Sam.

"Tazer make it to Nikolai all right?" Sam's voice sounded from behind her and Kat jumped.

She didn't realize how on edge she was until then. "Yes. She's going to check out all fuel sales and nose around for people coming in and out on snowmobiles. That won't be terribly easy, with so many people following the race at this point." She shook her head. There were always people coming and going on snowmobiles from the remote villages. In the winter, snowmobiles and small planes were the only forms of transportation available.

"Then let's get going."

Kat inhaled a deep breath and let it out. "This is perhaps one of the longest bad stretches of the trail. Be careful out there."

His lips quirked up on one side. "You, too."

Having been in this race more often than Sam, Kat took the lead.

Leaving the relative shelter of the spruce trees surrounding Rohn, she headed out onto the sandbars of the Kuskokwim River. Once she dropped down on the river, the wind hit Kat and her team like a freight train. Although the trail was wide-open, the riverbed was treacherous, with bare gravel, slick ice and areas of shallow open water.

Bent double to combat the wind, Kat had to get out in front of her lead dog several times to keep Loki headed in a southwesterly direction. Trail markers were few and far between. If she hadn't known that the course ran across the river and to the southwest, she might have gotten lost.

With forty-mile-per-hour winds and gusts up to sixty blowing easterly, she tugged at Loki's harness, urging him across the river, slipping and sliding, landing on her butt more than once. Thank goodness for the heavy layers of clothing cushioning her falls. Each time she landed on her radio, she cringed. She needed it to last the rest of the race for Sam.

When Kat glanced back, Sam's team followed close behind, leaning hard into the wind.

How were they supposed to find someone in trouble if they were too busy managing the trail themselves? Kat glanced around on more than one occasion, wondering if they were missing the clues.

She'd left her headlamp on even though sun still shone in the sky. The light from her headlamps eventually bounced off the reflective markers in the tree line near the river's edge, guiding her away from the wind tunnel of a riverbed. Back on the trail, her team climbed out of the river bottoms and up a ravine onto a plateau.

They traveled through the Buffalo Chutes, past Farewell Lake and across Farewell Burn, where over a million and a half acres of forest burned in the summer of 1978. The sun had set hours earlier, but moonlight helped guide them through the maze of trails. Six grueling hours on her feet, balancing the sled and urging her dogs on, were taking their toll on Kat.

Sam had assisted her when her sled tipped over on a couple of the icy areas and she'd helped him right his once.

She almost felt as if the race had settled back into nothing more than a race to the finish. But where was the threat their BG had alluded to? Had they completely missed it?

When Kat knew the dogs needed rest and she couldn't stand on the runners one minute longer, she spied the sign for the Bureau of Land Management's Bear Creek Cabin. With a sob of relief she yelled, "Gee!"

As if they knew they would be stopping soon, the dogs immediately obeyed and turned right up the trail to the bush-shelter cabin.

Kat parked her dogs in the space set aside for them and removed her stiff hands from the handlebar. Her entire body felt ramrod straight, as if, should she bend, she'd fall over like a log and never get up.

The dogs flopped down immediately, only to jump up again when Sam's sled slid in beside them.

Kat was so tired she wanted to cry. For a brief moment, she wished she wasn't an agent and just a girl so that she could have an emotional outburst without caring whether or not she let down her guard. But there were dogs to feed, water and bed down for several hours.

She removed the bale of straw from her sled and quietly went to work. Her team had worked far harder than she had. They deserved a break and food to keep up their energy.

Two other mushers had chosen the cabin for a rest stop, their teams already snuggled into their straw beds.

When Kat finally completed caring for the dogs, she entered the cabin. She moved around, quietly claiming the top bunk on the right side of the small room.

When she saw the yellow jacket hanging on a peg on the wall she didn't even have the energy to groan. Al Fendley. She hoped he didn't start bragging about how he'd win this race again. She'd just as soon punch him in the nose as look at him. After shedding her coat and boots, she was attempting to haul her exhausted body into the top bunk when Sam entered.

He crossed the room and placed a hand on her butt, shoving her up onto the top mattress where she collapsed, too tired to be embarrassed.

"Wake me in two hours," she said, hiding a hideously huge yawn behind her hand.

"I will."

Her eyes drifted closed. "What about BG's surprise problem?"

"BG?"

"Bad guy." Kat's eyes opened briefly.

Sam shook his head, a hint of a smile on his tired face. "The dogs need rest."

"I know. I just keep thinking…"

His hand smoothed the hair out of her face and cupped her chin. "Stop thinking for two hours and get some sleep. It'll be morning by then. We still have four more hours to Nikolai and Tazer."

He didn't have to say it twice. Exhaustion overruled guilt for not continuing the search. Sam had been right about her not being in shape for the race. Her shoulders, legs and back had taken a beating and she needed to lie in a prone position and slee…

Dreams didn't plague her nap, not even nightmares. Kat slept like the dead until her satellite phone vibrated against her side. She sat up in the bunk and grabbed for her jacket. On the fifth ring, she whispered, "Yeah?"

"It's me," Tazer said. "Where are you?"

Kat's sleep-numb brain grasped around the dark interior of the cabin and the foggy gray matter in her head for several seconds before she answered, "Bear Creek Cabin, about thirty miles from Nikolai."

Tazer spoke in a low voice, "I ran into Warren Fendley gassing up his snowmobile after dark. I followed him to the municipal building where he bedded down for the night. You following me?"

"I'm with you." Sort of. She needed coffee and a razor to scrape her teeth, but she was slowly coming awake.

The door to the cabin opened, blowing in a freezing blast of arctic air. Sam strode in with two canteen cups and a plastic bag of instant coffee. He leaned close, his breath feathering across her cheek. "That Tazer?"

Kat nodded, wide-awake. Heat suffused her face and neck, even as she shivered from the cold air penetrating her wool sweater and sock-covered feet.

"Anyway," Tazer continued, "he's headed out now and I'm following him."

Kat's hair had worked its way loose of the ponytail and fell over her face. She pushed it behind her ears, wondering how bad she must look and not caring enough to find a brush. "Which way is he going?"

"Your way."

Static crackled in Kat's ear. Tazer must have stepped out into the wind.

"He's leaving town now. I gotta go." Before Tazer hit the Off button, the sound of an engine revving reached Kat.

"What was that all about?" Sam poured hot water over instant coffee, the aroma filling the air of the snug little cabin.

"Tazer left Nikolai following Warren Fendley. He's headed our way." Kat slid over the side of the bunk, dropped to the floor in her socked feet.

Sam's hand steadied her. Then he handed her a cup of coffee.

"I could get used to having you around." She inhaled, letting the steam rise and warm her face, the rich aroma reviving her sluggish brain cells.

"You're not so bad yourself when you're not trying

to be all superior and tough." Sam swallowed liquid from his cup and nodded toward the empty bunks. "Al and the other guy left about an hour ago."

Kat frowned and glanced at her watch. Just as promised, Sam was on his way to wake her when Tazer called. Nothing like a man who kept his word. "They didn't stay long."

"Guess he wants to win this race. I followed him out."

"Don't trust him?"

"I don't trust anyone right now." His lips twitched. "Except maybe you."

"Maybe?" She marched up to him and poked a finger against his chest. "I've saved your butt on this trip a couple times already. I think you can trust me."

He grabbed her finger and held it, staring down into her eyes. "Did you know your eyes turn almost blue-green when you get all intense?"

His big calloused hand holding hers made her empty stomach flip-flop. "Don't change the subject." When she tried to pull her fingers loose, he held tighter.

"I wasn't." He turned her hand over and opened her palm, dropping a small disk into it.

The metal felt cool against her skin. "What's this?"

"Part of a tracking system." Sam's lips firmed. "Back on the trail when I was waiting for you before Rohn, something our BG said stuck with me. He knew we were almost to Rohn, but he talked as if he was farther along the trail."

Kat's eyes widened. "Where did you find this?"

"I started searching on the sled itself and ended up

digging into my supplies. I found it in the last food-drop bag we picked up at Rainy Pass." He nodded toward her jacket. "You better get dressed. I haven't been through your food bag, but I'd bet my best boots you have one of the same at the bottom of it."

"Son of a—"

"No kidding."

Her mind wrapped around the implications, the coffee jump-starting her brain out of the fog of sleep. "If we take them off, he'll know."

"Yeah, I say we keep them for a while, until we can come up with something to turn the tables on him."

"In the meantime, Tazer's out there."

Sam cupped her face with his palm. "Tazer's an S.O.S. agent, isn't she?"

Kat's skin tingled at the connection, but she didn't break free of his though. "Yes."

His thumb brushed across her cheek as he stared down at her lips. "She can take care of herself."

Kat's breath hung in her throat, refusing to push past to her lungs. Sam's lips were close enough to touch if she leaned forward a little. What was she thinking? Kat backed away until Sam's hand dropped. "Tazer doesn't know the terrain." She turned and paced across the tiny room and back. "She's never even been in Alaska before this."

"She's smart. She has to be for Royce to hire her."

She stopped in front of him, just out of his reach, her cheek still tingling from his contact. "I know, but she's my friend."

"And you don't want to lose another person you love."

Kat gazed into his eyes, hers suddenly filling. "What the heck's wrong with me?" She brushed away an errant tear falling down her cheek. "I never cry."

Sam reached out again. Tipping her face up, he rubbed his thumbs over the tears following the first one. "Maybe you should do it more often."

She wanted to lean her forehead into his chest and let Sam handle everything, shoulder the burden, make it all better. Instead, she brushed his hands aside. "I don't have that luxury. I have to get through this race alive. And now I have to get Tazer off the trail alive." She shrugged into her jacket and crammed her feet into her boots, tightening the laces with one yank on each side.

When she finally looked up, Sam was still staring at her.

"Know this, Kat. We'll make it through this race together. You and me. And we will help Tazer, as well. Like it or not, we're a team now."

A team. She hadn't been a team since Marty died. The idea of teaming with Sam felt good, but she didn't want to rely on anyone, especially someone she might come to care for. She wasn't going to stand around and argue.

"GOOD MORNING, Sam." A cheerful voice blasted into Sam's ear. "I might never get used to that. The man I'm going to kill is named Sam. Such an inconsequential name for a man who knows how to destroy another man's life, isn't it?"

Sam wanted to turn off the voice in his ear, but he

knew in order to draw him out, he had to play along. "You know my name, what's yours?"

"Uh-uh," he answered. "You have to figure that one out."

"Then tell me how I destroyed your life."

"In every way imaginable, Sam, my boy, that's how."

Sam's hands gripped the handlebar so tightly he thought it might bend and break. "What the hell do you want?"

"I met a friend of yours last night in Nikolai."

Sam knew Kat would be listening to the conversation, as well, and he could only imagine her reaction to this news.

"I don't know what you're talking about. I don't have any friends in Nikolai."

His voice turned harsh. "Come, Sam, don't think I'm a fool. She has blond hair and she's a knockout, even in her parka and snow pants. Where'd you find this one?"

He'd spotted Tazer. Tazer had mentioned seeing Warren Fendley last night and she was following him out of Nikolai. Was the man on the radio Warren? Was he the one who'd been tormenting him for the past couple of days?

"In fact, I see her now. My, my, she sure knows how to handle a snowmobile. Too bad she won't be handling it much longer."

Sam had been on the trail for less than two hours, which meant he should be getting near Tazer. If he hurried, he might intercept the BG's moves.

They'd just crossed nine miles of trail nearly obliterated by blowing snow, struggling the entire way to locate trail markers and engineering tape. Several times he lost sight of Kat. If Tazer was anywhere near, they might have missed her.

Was their BG in front of them or behind them?

When they entered the Salmon River fish camp, Sam pulled up next to Kat and yanked the protective earflaps from his ears so that he could listen.

For several seconds he didn't hear anything, the cold biting viciously at his earlobes.

Kat did the same and stood quietly, her head cocked to one side. "There, do you hear that?"

Sam nodded and turned, trying to get a bearing on the direction.

The sound grew louder until a snowmobile skidded around the corner of the trail to the north of where they stood.

Hot on the tail of the snowmobile was another.

"That has to be Tazer!" Kat shouted, scrambling to release her rifle from the scabbard on the side of her sled.

Before either one of them could free their weapons and aim, the two snowmobiles raced past. The front machine skidded around a tree and raced back the way they'd come, instead of turning north toward Nikolai, the lead snowmobile headed up the Salmon River.

"No!" Kat knew the river had open water in many places. At the speed the machines were traveling, the lead wouldn't see the open water or thin ice until it was too late.

Kat released her brake, pulled up her snow hook and shouted, "Let's go!" The dogs leaped forward, racing after the disappearing snowmobiles as if they could catch them. Kat wished they could. Otherwise she could be losing another one of the people she cared about.

Chapter Ten

The snowmobiles disappeared up the banks of the river and into the tree line. For a moment, Sam lost sight of them. Then Tazer shot over the top of the banks and slammed down the steep incline to the river. The other snowmobile stopped at the top.

Kat dug her foot brake into the snow and yelled to the team, "Whoa!"

The man straddling the snowmobile on the bank pulled out a rifle and lifted it to his shoulder. At first he turned toward Kat and Sam and aimed the weapon straight at Kat's chest.

"Get down, Kat!" Sam shouted into his mic.

Kat ducked behind the minimal cover of the supplies on her sled bag and peered around. "What's he doing?"

Sam didn't respond. He threw himself from the sled and rolled behind a nearby tree. Bark exploded from the trunk where his head would have been. His stomach clenched when the man aimed the rifle toward the snowmobile racing down the icy river.

A shot ripped through the frigid air.

Sam's breath lodged in his throat and he watched the scene unfold in front of him as if time had slowed.

The bullet didn't strike the rider, but a poof of powdery snow rose from the ice several yards in front of her.

"No!" Kat left the cover of her sled and ran forward. "Get off the ice!" she yelled, waving her rifle. But the rider couldn't hear her and kept going, right into the trap the man had set.

Dropping to one knee, Sam braced his rifle against his shoulder and sighted down the barrel, anger steadying his hand. As he squeezed the trigger, the man on the snowmobile spun in a circle and disappeared into the trees. Completely disappeared.

The snowmobile on the river slowed too late, skidding sideways, unable to stop the forward momentum on the ice. Beneath the machine, the frozen river buckled and large chunks of ice dipped, the snowmobile sliding right in, rider and all.

Sam dug inside his sled bag for the length of rope he carried with him for just such an emergency. Kat emerged with her own rope. They'd need both to fish Tazer out of the river. Assuming they caught her before she slipped beneath the ice. Hypothermia would set in quickly and she wouldn't remain afloat very long.

Leaving his team behind, Sam raced along the riverbank until he was parallel with where the snowmobile had gone under. Tazer's head bobbed up in the water.

"Hang on, Tazer!" Sam tied the rope to a tree and hurried down the bank.

Kat beat him to the river's edge.

The woman in the water clung to the edge of the unbroken ice, her lips turning blue, her movements slowing. "D-damn cold," she said. Her teeth chattered so hard, Sam was afraid they'd chip.

"Wait, Kat." Sam eased onto the ice behind her.

"She'll die if we don't get her out."

"I know, let me have your rope." He tied his own strand to the end of Kat's rope. "Let me go out. You stay here and pull us back if the ice shelf breaks."

"No. You're too heavy. Let me."

"She'll be deadweight," he said softly. "Can you carry yourself and another body out?"

Kat stared from him to Tazer. She stepped back, making a knot in the end of the rope before handing it to him. "Go get her. I'll watch your back."

Sam tied the rope around his waist and eased out on the ice, dropping into a low crawl. The more spread-eagle he was on the ice, the less pressure he exerted in any particular spot.

Ominous cracking sounds didn't make him feel any better, but he kept his focus on his goal.

"H-hurry…it…up…c-cowboy." Tazer's words slurred and her hands slipped from the ice. Her head dipped below the surface.

Sam made a grab for her fingers, snagging them before they disappeared beneath the dark waters.

Holding on to her hand, Sam pulled Tazer back to the surface. With Kat tugging the rope from behind, Sam scooted back on the ice, pulling the limp woman with him, until she slid out of the water onto the ice.

"Pull, Kat, pull," Sam yelled.

Kat wrapped the rope around her waist and backed up the bank, leaning into the effort with all her strength.

When he felt the surface was strong enough, Sam climbed to his knees, swooped Tazer up in his arms and raced across the ice to the shore. With every step the ice fractured more beneath his feet, but it held until he made it to safety.

Tazer laid against his chest, her face pale and her lips a deathly shade of purple.

"We have to get her to the fish-camp cabin." Kat's voice was low and urgent.

Sam strode back the way they'd come, laying Tazer across the top of his sled. Kat grabbed the lead's harness and turned the team in a tight circle until they faced back toward the camp.

"Let's go!" Sam called out and the team leaped forward.

Kat turned her team and threw herself on the runners as her lead followed the other sled up the banks to the camp.

Inside the cabin, Kat made quick work of stripping Tazer while Sam stoked the potbellied stove and started a fire.

He left the cabin and returned with his sleeping bag and dry clothing. "Here, get her into this."

Together, they dressed Tazer in dry clothes and rolled her into the sleeping bag, zipping it all the way up. Then they sandwiched her between them and sat her close to the growing fire, rubbing her arms and legs through the thick bag.

Soon she was shaking so hard her teeth rattled against each other.

Sam went back out to gather the cooker, a pan and coffee fixings to help Tazer warm up inside, as well.

The sassy blonde, with attitude to spare, perked up when she smelled coffee. "If I'd known all I had to do was go swimming with the polar bears to get a cup of coffee, I'd have done it sooner." The teeth rattling between words watered down her sarcasm, but her sarcasm was a very good sign.

"Are you warming up finally?" Kat brushed limp blond hair from her friend's face.

"I don't think I'll ever be warm again." Her body shook beneath the sleeping bag. "What I wouldn't give to take a two-by-four to that bastard."

"You and me both." Sam held a canteen cup full of hot coffee up to her lips. "Drink this. It'll help with the chills."

"Ah, the elixir of the gods." Leaning against Kat, Tazer sipped the warm liquid, her eyes closing for a moment. When she opened them again, she stared up at Sam. "So why the hell did you quit the S.O.S.?"

Not expecting the question, Sam stared at her for a moment before answering. "It's not something I like to talk about."

"Got nothing else to do out here." Her body trembled and her teeth clamped together.

Sam held the cup away from her until the tremors slowed. "You could concentrate on warming up."

She grabbed for the cup and held it between her hands before saying softly, "We all make mistakes."

"Not ones involving the death of a child." Sam turned away and shoved another log into the wood-burning stove, regretting his words.

"You c-can't leave us hanging after a statement like that," Tazer said, her voice still shaky but getting closer to her normal to-the-point agent inquisition.

"Finish the coffee. I'll get the other sleeping bag from Kat's sled. That should keep you warm until we get to Nikolai."

Tazer stared at him across the top of the canteen cup. "And I thought we were getting somewhere." Thankfully, she didn't pursue her interrogation. Sam bet she'd call Royce and fish for more at the first opportunity.

Back out in the bitter cold, Sam scanned the area for their BG.

"Did you get a make on the snowmobile?" Kat appeared beside him, zipping her jacket and pulling the hood up around her ears.

"Yeah. Looked like a Polaris, black with gray flames on the sides."

She sighed. "Sounds like at least half the models sold in Alaska. What are the chances of identifying our BG by the snowmobile he drives?"

"Slim to none." Sam dug in Kat's sled for her sleeping bag. "Let's set Tazer up in your sled. You weigh less than I do."

"Okay. Give us fifteen minutes and we'll be ready."

Kat reentered the cabin, closing the door behind her.

She'd been courageous and fully engaged in this race for life. Sam couldn't ask for a better partner or a more trustworthy one. Kat cared about her family, as evidenced by her concern for her brother. She also had extended family at the S.O.S. agency she cared for just as much. Somehow, she'd included him in that extended family, looking out for him, as well as Tazer.

The thought of either one of the women getting hurt because their BG wanted him ate at Sam's gut. When he got to Nikolai, he had an idea of something he could do about it.

THE SMALL TOWN of Nikolai lay on the banks of the Kuskokwim River with an airstrip, a small school and several buildings scattered around the flat landscape. The area was a circus of mushers and dogs. By now the animals were tired and dropped to their straw beds, ready to rest and soak up the warm sunshine glaring off the snow.

Kat helped Tazer to the local school where she was able to obtain more dry clothing while she washed and dried her own. A villager loaned her a sleeping bag and a cot where she could rest up from her near miss with death. She insisted she'd be back up to snuff within the hour.

Kat disagreed.

After what her team had to endure with the extra load and pushing through many rest breaks, Kat declared they'd take an eight-hour rest. Then she got down to the business of feeding and checking each of her animals, massaging sore muscles and working with the veterinarian to identify those needing a free ride back to Anchorage. Shamus, one of her wheel dogs, didn't look well and hadn't eaten since Rainy Pass. Kat medicated him and dropped him from the team. He'd done well so far, no use pushing him if he wasn't up to it.

Hot water was readily available and Kat mixed up warm bowls of liver and high-protein dog food for her team.

Once they were bedded down, Kat looked forward to a real bathroom and a shower in the school gym.

Sam joined her on the walk toward the school. "I need to talk to Royce. Mind if I borrow your satellite phone?"

Kat slid the phone to him, keeping it out of sight. "Get an ETA on Valdez and McNeal, will ya? Right now, I know there's a shower in that building with my name on it. I'll shoot anyone who gets in my way." She left him standing in the sunshine without a backward glance.

Toiletries and fresh clothing in hand, Kat entered the gym and immediately bumped into Al and Warren Fendley. Just her lousy luck.

"Heard you ran into a little trouble back near the fish camp." Al's voice boomed in the hallway, attracting the attention of others passing through.

Kat paused, staring more at Warren than Al. "Yeah, so?" In a small town, she wasn't surprised the word had gotten around so quickly. The doctor who'd checked

Tazer out had asked a lot of questions. Others had been nearby to hear the answers. With so many people in and around the facilities, privacy was at a premium.

"Gotta be careful out there on the trail." Al's eyes narrowed at Kat. "Never know what you're gonna run into."

Kat's brows rose and she gave Al and Warren pointed looks. "Not just what, but who. Should I be afraid?"

"Possibly."

She crossed her arms over her chest and glared at both of them. "Well, I'm not."

"I like to win, Ms. Sikes," Al said. "Make no mistake about that. I won't let anyone get in the way of what I want."

"Then win because you deserve it, not because you eliminate the competition, Mr. Fendley. Now, get out of my way."

Al's eyes narrowed into slits. "Who said anything about eliminating the competition? You think you're all that?" He shoved her, pinning her shoulders to the wall. "I'll win this race and nothing you or Russell can do will stop me. Same goes for that oil deal. It'll happen, no matter what Russell tries to tell those suits in Washington. He just better watch himself, he's making some powerful enemies."

Anger simmered just beneath the surface, and Kat's lip pulled back in a snarl. "Get your hands off me, Mr. Fendley."

"Or what?" He leaned close, his bad breath gagging Kat.

She raised her hands in a sharp movement, knocking his hands from her shoulders. At the same time, her knee connected to his groin in a hard knock to his sensitive parts.

Al doubled over, all the air sucked from his lungs.

A scowl thundered across Warren's forehead and he stepped forward, his hands rising to grab Kat.

"Touch me and I'll make you hurt worse than your brother."

His eyes narrowed and he moved nearer, glancing down at his brother who'd collapsed against the wall. He hesitated, the skin on his face turning red and blotchy.

"You want to rumble, come on." Kat beckoned him closer with a flick of her fingers. "I could use a little exercise."

People pushed past them in the hallway, but Kat didn't remove her gaze from her quarry. He might attack when she had her guard down. Warren looked like that kind of fighter. He also looked as if he wouldn't hesitate to hit a woman.

Good. Kat would love an excuse to take the big bad Fendleys down. If they were in any way responsible for the attacks on Sam, George and Tazer, she'd nail their butts to the wall, no questions asked. Her eyes must have narrowed, maybe steam rose from her collar, she didn't know, but Warren ended the staring game first.

Al staggered to his feet. "Don't get in my way, Sikes. They shouldn't have even let you in this race. I have a mind to question the officials and have you disqualified."

"You don't scare me with your threats. Why don't you try winning a race based on your skills just once, rather than relying on your brother to manhandle you through?" She knew she was pushing, but if he was cheating, he'd get caught sooner or later. Maybe her questions would flush him out sooner.

Warren stepped closer, glaring down his fat, flaring nostrils at her. "Don't go spreadin' no rumors you can't substantiate, little girl. You'll find yourself in deeper water than your friend and no one there to fish you out."

"Is that a threat, Mr. Fendley?"

"No. I'll make that a promise."

A tremor of fear snaked down Kat's back and for a moment she could picture Warren as the rider on the snowmobile today. As mean-spirited as he was, he could easily have chased Tazer into the river and then shot the ice out from under her. He and his brother ran a hunting-outfitter business, they owned multiple snowmobiles and they certainly knew their way around guns.

"Kat, there you are." Sam stepped into the hallway, his gaze sweeping over the two men standing so close to her. "These guys bothering you?"

"Not at all, nor will they." She raised a challenging eyebrow.

"Good. I need to talk to you." He hooked her elbow and led her outside.

So much for showering and brushing her teeth.

"I don't want to stay here too long. There are too

many people. If our BG is here, we'd never pick him out. I say we move on through McGrath to Takotna before we stop for our twenty-four-hour rest. It means he'd have to camp out if he doesn't want to be caught."

"We have to let the dogs rest at least another two hours before we move on. Sheba and Fabio aren't eating and Toby's favoring his wrists. They need rest."

"I know. I had to drop Hammy for a sore shoulder. I promise we'll stop for an entire day. I want to get past the media circus in case he decides to play his hand in front of them."

"Good point." She sighed. The thought of waiting another seven or eight hours before a shower and clean clothing nearly made her cry. The thought that their bad guy might make a move in a crowded town didn't make her any more comfortable. "Okay. But not for another two hours." No matter how badly they needed to go, the dogs could only take so much. Given their own choice, they'd run until they dropped dead.

Kat found Tazer in the community center stretched out on a cot, smothered in sleeping bags. She lay down on the cot next to her and turned to face her friend. "Are you doing okay?"

Tazer nodded, her blond hair dry and messy around her face and no makeup to coat her perfect skin. Kat hadn't seen her so natural, well, ever. It made Tazer look like a little lost girl, not the tough S.O.S. agent she always portrayed. The fact that one dunking in a potentially deadly river could shake her stoic friend so much had Kat doubting her own abilities.

"Don't look so glum. I'm fine." She pushed up on an elbow. "If you two need to get going, do it. I'll be all right in a few hours and back on the trail as soon as I can find another snowmobile to rent."

"Do you think anyone would rent a snowmobile to you after you ditched the last one in the river?" Kat chuckled. "I know I wouldn't."

Tazer's brows dipped into a pretty frown. "I hadn't thought of that."

"I don't want you to follow us, Tazer. When Sam and I leave, stay here. If I know you're on the trail, I'll lose my focus worrying about you."

Tazer attempted to sit up, struggling to push aside the sleeping bags. "I'm not a sissy girl to be pampered and looked after." Her body shook with a violent quiver and she hiked a bag up to her shoulders. "I'm just cold. I'll be fine in a few minutes."

"You took a dip in freezing water. You're still suffering the aftereffects of hypothermia. I'd feel better knowing you aren't out there getting cold all over again."

"I'm going."

"No. You're not. If I have to call Royce to pull rank, I will."

A muscle twitched in Tazer's rigid jawline. "You're a pushy broad, you know that?" She snuggled back into her sleeping bag and zipped it to her chin.

Kat smiled. "I learned from the best."

Tazer's slim brows rose with their usual sophisticated flair. "And don't you forget it."

Kat lay back on the cot. "Mind if I catch a few Z's?"

"Go ahead. I've got your back."

With one last jaw-splitting yawn, Kat closed her eyes and fell to sleep.

SAM WAITED until Kat had settled in at the community center before he walked back out to make that call to Royce. He had something to ask he didn't want Kat to hear. Not yet.

Royce answered the satellite phone after only one ring. "Kat?"

"No, this is Sam."

"Did you meet up with Tazer in Nikolai?"

"As a matter of fact, we fished her out of the water near the Salmon River fish camp."

"Alive?" Royce's voice sounded strained and concerned.

"Yes, alive, but shaken."

The older man sighed. "Tell me about it."

After debriefing his former boss, Sam asked, "Have you learned anything more about the oil issue?"

"Nothing. But Blalock is on his way back to Alaska, as we speak."

"So soon? I would have thought he'd stay until I showed up in D.C. to give them my findings in two weeks."

"Maybe he thinks you're not going to be giving that briefing after all," Royce suggested. "None of my contacts can tell me whether or not Blalock put a contract out on you. If he did, he pulled it off in Alaska or somewhere outside of D.C."

"If he's contracted someone, I get the feeling whoever it is has a bigger beef with me than the oil issues in this state."

"What are you thinking?"

"Check with the Saudi government. I want to know the current status of a certain prisoner."

"Bradley English?"

"He's been known to finagle his way out of tight situations. Who's to say he didn't make a deal with the devil to get off murder charges?"

"I'll get right on it. Might take a little time to find the inside information. We don't have anyone over there right now."

"Time is something I don't have a lot of. This guy went after Tazer. He might go after Kat next." The thought made his belly clench. "I won't let that happen. She's been through enough already."

"Kat's a professional—"

"I know, I know. She can take care of herself."

"But you'd rather she didn't have to."

"Exactly. Whoever has a gripe has it with me. As soon as I can, I'm going to do something about it."

"In the meantime, I'll check into this. There are a couple people in Riyadh who owe me a favor or two."

"Whatever it takes. I need to know Brad's whereabouts. This guy is smart and stays one step ahead."

"Just like Brad?"

"Yeah." How else could he have fooled Sam so easily? That, and he'd trusted Brad as part of his team.

"Everyone has a weakness and even smart people make mistakes."

Sam's jaw clenched. "I'm going to be there when he makes his."

"Valdez and McNeal just landed in Anchorage. Where do you want them to meet up with you?"

"Fly them in to Ruby. We're on our way out of Nikolai in an hour or two. I want to keep this guy moving to lessen his chance of hurting any racers."

"Good idea," Royce agreed. "I'll send them to Ruby and have them work their way backward down the trail."

"That works. The trail should be no problem from there. Tell them to keep radio traffic to a minimum. I don't want our bogey to know they're out there." Sam gave Royce a radio frequency for Valdez and McNeal to use when they neared the checkpoint at Ophir. "Kat and I are moving on to McGrath for our twenty-four-hour rest. We should be there in about seven hours."

"I'll try to have something for you by then, but no guarantees." Royce would pull every string and call in all his favors to determine Bradley English's whereabouts and get that information back to Sam. As the head of the S.O.S., he was one of the best. As a person, he was even better.

And here he was, on the last frontier and trouble had managed to follow him practically to the end of the earth. Sam rang off and tromped through the snow to look after his dogs and find another cup of coffee. The next several hours would be long. And what he planned to do in McGrath wouldn't win any new friendships between him and Kat.

Chapter Eleven

After six hours on the trail, Kat's hands and legs were numb. Even her brain was numb. The dogs were slowing and needed a full day's rest and plenty of good food.

They hadn't heard from their BG since Tazer took a swim in the Salmon River.

Speaking of Tazer, she hadn't been all that happy when they'd sent her back to Anchorage on an airplane with the dogs they'd dropped from the race.

The fact that they hadn't heard from the BG had Kat wondering whether her headset was broken from all the spills she'd taken. Every once in a while, Sam's voice sounded in her ear, soothing her fraying nerves. If this race had done one thing, it had made her rely on him for mental support, if nothing else. Kat liked having him as a trail partner. She liked helping him out of trouble and having him around to help her. Almost too much. His quiet determination and strength touched her like the majesty of the Alaska Range. He was the kind of guy she could see always being there when you needed him.

Why she should think that, she didn't know. Not with a madman after him on the trail. Yet, Sam took everything in stride and kept moving forward.

This trip had shown Kat that, whether you wanted it to or not, life moved on. And she should continue to move forward just like Sam. Otherwise she'd miss out on her chance for happiness again.

Was Sam part of that happiness? Did she want him to be? With too many empty hours to pass on the trail, she'd had more than her share of time to think it over and she still didn't have the answer.

The road into McGrath was hard and fast, traversing the frozen Kuskokwim River. Pushing toward the sky to her right was the Kuskokwim hills, nothing but a deep shadow in the light from the moon. Snow blew across the river in a low fine powder, giving the appearance of a rising mist.

This country was truly beautiful, and nothing angered Kat more than when someone ruined her enjoyment of that beauty by threatening to take the lives of innocents. When she and Sam reached McGrath, they had to put their heads together and come up with a plan to draw out their BG and put an end to the torment. They had to go on the offensive rather than being in the reactionary mode all the time.

"Miss me?" The voice in Kat's ear wasn't Sam's. It was the voice she'd come to dread more with each passing hour and day. She wanted to answer him by cursing him up one side and down the other, but Sam insisted they limit all communication to just Sam and the BG, to minimize his connection to Kat. Like that would make him forget Kat, and she could disappear.

Kat wished her Mute button wasn't activated. She'd tell him how much she missed him.

"Your blond friend was good, but not good enough, was she?"

"This has got to end," Sam's voice cut into their BG's laughter.

"Oh, it will, my friend, it will." All laughter died and his voice grew as cold as a blue norther blowing across the tundra. "When I say it ends. In the meantime, I'm having too much fun keeping you guessing. Because you are guessing, aren't you?"

Sam didn't answer, the silence lengthening between them.

"How about you, Ms. Sikes?" he asked. "Or should I call you Kat? Meow. I like that. Makes me want to rub up against you."

A shiver of revulsion ran across Kat's skin. She'd rather curl up with a rattlesnake and she would have told him as much, but that would be playing into his sick little game.

"Not long until you make McGrath. Maybe I'll see you there."

Kat wished she and Sam could talk over the radio.

As if reading her mind, Sam slowed his sled in front of her until her dogs slid in beside his on the river. "Whoa!"

Together, they brought their teams to a halt.

"You heard him, he'll be in McGrath." Kat tapped her fingers against the handlebar. "What can we do to catch him there without someone else getting hurt?"

"That's one of the busiest checkpoints on the route.

He could easily slip in unnoticed. There'll be spectators and media en masse along with all of the racers and checkpoint officials. It'll be impossible to pick him out."

"Damn. If the dogs didn't need their rest, I'd say let's push on, but mine are all slowing down and some of them are showing signs of wrist and shoulder soreness. If they don't get a long rest, they won't make it much farther. Much as I'd like to make Takotna before we stop, the dogs can't take it."

"Agreed. We'll have to make McGrath our stop. Hopefully, he won't pull anything with that many people around."

A lump of dread settled in the pit of Kat's stomach. "Let's hope not."

DESPITE THE CHEERFUL greeting provided by the residents of McGrath, Kat couldn't raise enough energy to feel happy. Having made it past the majority of the nasty mountainous trails and switchbacks, she should be elated, but she wasn't. Her nerves were stretched to the max, having watched for anything strange or unusual for the past few days.

A hot shower, hot food and a place to lie down were what she needed. Then she and Sam would figure out what to do about their BG. They were two smart agents—so Sam was an *ex*-agent. Between the two of them, they would come up with a plan.

An hour and a half later, after feeding, massaging and medicating her dogs, she tucked them into beds of straw and threw blankets over each one. Then she applied new runners to her sled, after the originals took a beating over the snowless rocky patches in the trail.

When her sled was ready and her dogs were fast asleep, Kat gathered her toiletries and the fresh clothing stashed in her food drop. *Thank you, Paul.* With coins in hand, she headed for the municipal building and the coin-operated shower inside the Laundromat.

She practically glared at every person who passed, wondering if the stranger's face she was peering into was the man causing them so much grief.

Sam was waiting his turn outside the shower facility when Kat came out. "Feel better?"

"Incredibly." She smiled for the first time in days, amazed at what a clean body and clean hair could do to raise her spirits. "See ya in the chow hall."

Kat sniffed her way to the kitchen where a full-time cook stood ready to grant her culinary wishes. Kat wanted to hug her for suggesting eggs, bacon and sausage. Too tired to make a decision as big as what to eat, she couldn't imagine staying awake long enough do it. "Could you make it two plates just like that?"

The lady gave her a friendly smile. "Sure."

While Kat waited for the food to cook, she filled a cup full of freshly brewed coffee and sat down at one of the tables.

A man sat across the table from her, carrying his own cup of coffee and sporting a wide grin. "You're one of the racers, aren't you? Katherine Sikes, right?"

Considering they'd shown her face over the news when running all the contestants' biographies, he'd have to be a fool or one of the media crawling throughout the checkpoints looking for a story.

Too tired for conversation, Kat lifted her lips briefly in a half smile. "That would be correct."

"I've always admired the mushers who enter this race. It must be quite a challenge, both mentally and physically."

"Yes, it is."

The man wasn't bad-looking. He actually didn't really look like a cameraman or newsman with his broad shoulders and chiseled features. He was nice-looking in a rugged way, like he should be out there mushing, not asking dumb questions. Medium-brown hair lay in tousled waves, a lock drooping down over his forehead. His eyes were a deep brown, almost black, and they twinkled when he spoke as if he was thinking of a joke he wasn't going to share. "I imagine there's an element of danger out there."

"A bit."

"It must be exciting." The man was digging, and Kat didn't feel like talking with him.

"Yeah, exciting." Kat sighed. She wished she had half his energy. Standing on the back of a sled for hours on end took a lot out of her. Plus the added stress of worry about that "element of danger" made her exhausted. "Look, I'm really tired and I might just fall asleep before my food is ready."

"Two eggs, overeasy, bacon and sausage?"

Kat gave the man a weak smile. "That's my call. Excuse me." She stood, walked to the counter and collected her plate of food.

Sam entered just then, his sandy-blond hair wet and his face shiny clean. "Mmm, that smells like heaven."

Kat grinned and handed him the plate she carried. "You're just in time."

He hesitated, refusing to take the plate. "Isn't this yours?"

"I had her make it a double." She glanced around, looking for her unwanted friend. Where he'd been a moment before, the seat was empty. All that was left was her disposable coffee cup. Kat frowned. She must have been crabbier than she thought. Not that she wanted to sit with him, but the now-you-see-me-now-you-don't trick was a bit unnerving.

"Something wrong?" Sam asked.

Kat shook her head. "No, not at all. I'm just hungry." She settled her plate on the table and sat.

"Coffee?"

Her gaze went to the cup she'd left on the other table. A volunteer, armed with a rag, made quick work of wiping the surface and clearing the cup. "Sure."

Sam retrieved two cups from the coffee urn and they ate in silence, enjoying the first hot meal they'd had in days.

When the last crumb was gone from her plate, Kat leaned back in her chair and wrapped her hands around her warm cup. The aroma alone would normally revive her, but she was too tired. "Want to discuss a plan?" she asked, brushing a drying tendril from her face.

"You look too tired to discuss anything but how long it'll take to find a cot or mattress."

"True." She set her cup on the table and leaned her chin in the palm of her hand, fighting the weight of her eyelids. "We can't let him keep us reacting. We have to get ahead of him, lure him out and make him come to us." Okay, even if her eyelids were closed, she could still listen and get through this planning stage.

A large calloused hand reached across the table and cupped the other side of her face not already resting in her hand.

Kat's eyes fluttered open and she stared into Sam's warm green gaze.

"We'll talk later. Right now, you need sleep."

"But what about our BG?" She yawned, her face heating with embarrassment.

"We're surrounded by a lot of people. Hopefully, he won't make a move with so many witnesses." Sam stood and rounded the table.

"Have you heard any news on George Engle?" Kat asked as he pulled her to her feet.

They stood so close she could feel the heat radiating from the solid wall of his chest. All she wanted to do was crawl into a sleeping bag with Sam and snuggle... naked.

Kat's eyes popped open, her gaze climbing up his broad chest to his sexy, stubbled chin. She stopped at his lips, afraid to meet his gaze, scared spitless he'd read her mind. Where had that thought come from? She and Sam were in a race for their lives, she didn't have time to think about getting naked with anyone.

But the image was now firmly rooted in her mind and

she couldn't shake it. The thought of sliding her body against his, skin to skin, sent sizzling tremors throughout her body.

He grabbed her hand and moved toward the door. "Come on, let's go find a bed."

Thank goodness the only place to rest was in a completely safe sleeping room where all the other mushers making this their twenty-four-hour rest stop slept. In a crowded room full of exhausted people, Kat wouldn't have to worry about this urge to be with Sam. It must be the fatigue crumbling her wall of reason. If she'd been back in D.C. or even in Anchorage, she wouldn't be having these thoughts about Sam Russell.

His arm circled her waist and he pulled her against his side as they exited the kitchen and went in search of the sleeping room. The gesture was one her brother might have used, knowing she was worn out.

They made one last check on the dogs to ensure they were okay and warm beneath their straw and blankets. Kat and Sam gathered sleeping bags and headed for the sleeping room.

Though her thoughts about Sam roiled around her head, she didn't protest when he lay on the cot next to hers. Nor did she protest when he reached out for her hand and held it until her eyelids would no longer cooperate. She couldn't fight it anymore. She slept.

How long she slept, Kat didn't know, but when she woke, it was morning. Meaning she'd slept more than ten hours. The cot next to hers was empty, the sleeping bag gone and Sam nowhere to be seen.

All sleepiness disappeared and she sat up straight. Where was Sam? She shoved her feet into her boots and began rolling her sleeping bag with quiet efficiency, careful not to wake the sleeping mushers.

Beneath her bag was a folded sheet of paper with her name written in bold letters across the top. A lump worked its way up from her chest into her throat and she sat on the edge of the cot, her knees suddenly weak. In the dim light from the sun coming through a window, she read.

Dear Kat,
I'm moving on in hopes I can draw out our BG. I put your GPS device on the airplane headed back to Anchorage. Since I'm the one he wants, I'm going farther along the trail to draw him out away from others. Don't follow me. You're in more danger by yourself than if you stay at the checkpoint, or better yet, go back to Anchorage. I'll see you at your brother's house in a few days.
Love, Sam.

Kat balled the note in her fist, the hard lump in her throat choking her as tears welled in her eyes. How could he do it? How could he go on without her? The BG was a maniac. He'd kill Sam now that he was out there on his own.

She reminded herself that Sam knew how to take care of himself. He'd be fine. Deep down, she couldn't accept that line of reasoning. The Iditarod was not the place to go it totally alone. Not with a killer after you. Sam needed backup.

Kat stood, anger fueling her movements. Sam Russell might think she needed protection, but he needed it more. He had another thing coming if he thought she'd sit back and do nothing.

SAM KNEW he'd defied the rules of the Iditarod by cutting his twenty-four-hour rest short, but he couldn't continue to place Kat at risk, not after what had happened to Tazer. Before daylight, he'd slipped out of the sleeping room and fed and watered his dogs, preparing for the trip ahead. He'd dropped Blitz, whose wrists still bothered him, but he still had fourteen healthy dogs to continue this insane race.

Before he left, he'd found the pilot of the airplane preparing to take off with a couple dogs headed back to Anchorage. He'd asked him to deliver a note to Paul Jenkins. Inside the envelope, he'd tucked the tracking device that had been in Kat's sled.

Hopefully, the BG wasn't really in McGrath as he'd threatened and, if he was, Sam hoped that if he got going quickly enough, he'd choose to follow Sam's tracking device instead of the one on the airplane.

Sam hurried back to his sled after he made one last pass down the line of dogs. "Let's go!"

The checkpoint handlers assisted him, lining him up to leave by way of the ramp angling down to the Kuskokwim River. Once on the river, the dogs took off, primed from their ten hours of rest.

Sam had switched off Kat's headset before he left. Now he switched his Mute off, but he waited until he was several miles away from McGrath before he checked in with the BG. "Hey, jerk-face, you awake?"

For a long minute, Sam held his breath, waiting for a response. Had he made a mistake? Was the BG still back in McGrath sleeping in? Would he take advantage of Sam being gone to get to Kat?

About to berate himself for being all kinds of a fool, Sam almost slammed on the foot brake and turned around when static preceded the voice that drew anger from him. "It's not nice to call people names."

Ignoring his comment, Sam got to the point. "I'm on the trail and my girlfriend is on the plane back to Anchorage. Come on. Catch me if you can."

"You knew the rules. You were both supposed to stay in the race."

"Look, you have me on your own. Come and get me."

A long breath sounded in Sam's ear.

"Too bad, someone has to die because you couldn't follow the rules."

"In the meantime, I'm way ahead of you on the trail and I don't think you have the guts to face me alone. You're a coward." He hoped that by pushing the BG with his taunts he would make him come after him.

"You're the coward, Sam, make no mistake about that. I was hired to do one thing and I will complete my task. Not for the money, but for the satisfaction of watching you die."

His taunting had paid off, if only a little. At least now,

Sam knew the BG had been hired to kill him. "Who paid you to kill me?"

"You're not as smart as you think, are you? Haven't figured it out yet?" The man laughed in Sam's ear. "Too bad. Now…who shall I kill?"

All the air left Sam's lungs. His plan had backfired. "I know you planted a GPS device on me. If you don't come after me now, you're going to lose me, because I'll drop it. Then you'll never catch me. You'll blow your mission and you won't get paid for killing me."

"You do that, and I'll kill contestants."

"Go ahead," Sam bluffed. "I don't know or care about them. And before long, I'll be miles away where you can't find me. Tell me, do you get paid if you don't deliver?"

A long pause followed Sam's goading and the BG said, "I know what you're trying to pull and it won't work."

"Fine by me. I'm dropping the GPS now and I'm turning off the radio. See if you can catch me now."

Sam switched his headset to Mute and fished the GPS device out of his coat pocket. "Here's to you, you murdering son-of-a—"

Holding on to the handlebar with one hand, he threw the GPS tracking device with the other.

The man blasted into Sam's ear. "I know you're still listening. I'll kill someone, just you watch."

Sam didn't respond. He hoped his plan worked. This way he had destroyed the BG's control. Maybe that would be enough to draw him away from Kat and the other contestants. He'd taken a gamble and he hoped it paid off, otherwise someone would die.

KAT CONFERRED with the checkpoint officials. Sam had left an hour before she did. One hour gave him a huge head start. She'd switched her headset on as soon as she'd figured out Sam had switched it off. Luckily, she'd caught the entire conversation between Sam and the BG. It had been enough to make her blood run cold.

Was the killer already on the trail? Or was he in one of the populated areas trying to decide who to pick off in retaliation for Sam and Kat splitting up?

The way Sam taunted him, Kat hoped the hell the BG would leave the contestants out of his plans for Sam and get back on the trail.

Anger fueled Kat's race now. Sam had no right to leave her behind. Despite what Sam might think, the geologist-slash-former-agent wasn't invincible. He needed a partner to watch his back. He needed her.

Or was it she needed him?

And, not only had he left her, he'd taken her satellite phone.

Clouds tumbled in over the horizon pregnant with snow, as if awaiting some invisible signal to let loose. The weather bulletin hadn't boded well for the mushers. A blizzard was predicted within the next couple hours, lasting throughout the rest of the day and the night ahead. Racing officials warned mushers to stay in a settlement if at all possible or hunker down in a sheltered area if they were caught out in the storm.

Ahead of the front, the temperatures were still a balmy minus ten. When the blizzard hit, the windchill would couple with lower air temperatures to make for a miserable night.

Through the trees of the swamp she traveled, Kat saw a bright flash of yellow.

Could it be Al Fendley?

With the only sound that of the runners sliding across the snow, Kat heard the gunshots clearly.

Her dogs jumped and dodged to the side as if the shots were being fired at them. Loki barked and settled back into leading the team when no other gunfire cracked the crisp, frigid air.

With a cold wash of dread icing her insides, Kat shouted to the team, "Go! Go! Go!"

Kat rounded a rise, her heart leaping into her throat.

Ahead, Al Fendley slumped over his handlebar and his sled listed to the side. With his body weight leaning to the right, the sled skidded across the snow and slammed into a spruce tree. The man bounced against the trunk and flopped to the ground, pulling the sled over onto its side. Al's trouser leg was caught on the sled, dragging him behind the team on his back.

If the bullets didn't kill him, being dragged along the rough terrain would. A smeared red trail fanned out on the snow behind the sled.

Kat yelled at the dogs, urging them faster. "Let's go!"

Loki lunged forward and the others followed. To them this was all part of the race, part of the competition, being the leaders of the packs.

With no brakes to slow them down, the dogs pulled their hardest, slowly catching up to the overturned sled.

Loki stayed the course, passing the man flopping over every tussock and rock on the ground. Several of the other dogs jerked to the side, eyeing the unusual sight, afraid of the flapping arms.

Al's team ran on, unaware their musher wasn't in control and possibly frightened by the sled slamming against the trees.

The trail narrowed and Kat was forced to drop back. At this rate, she'd never pull ahead of Al's team. They'd run on until they reached the Takotna checkpoint.

Ahead, the trail widened into a wide frozen swamp almost a mile long. A dark shadowy figure emerged from the tree line. Another musher headed her way, going the wrong direction on the trail. Even before she could see the red of his jacket, she knew it was Sam and she almost sagged against her handlebar. She reached up and switched her headset microphone on. "Stop the sled, Sam."

Sam didn't respond to her entreaty. Over the sound of the two sleds bumping across buffalo grass buried beneath the ice and snow, the sound of Sam yelling "Gee!" reached Kat.

His team turned in a wide arc, forming a line of dogs in front of the team racing out of control.

Kat's team pulled in beside Al's and she yelled loud enough for both to hear. "Whoa!"

Easing her sled closer to the injured man's sled, Kat stretched her leg as far as she could reach and stomped Al's brake. "Whoa!" She jerked his snow hook out of its catch and slammed it into the ground.

With her own sled wobbling and rocking side to side,

Kat leaned back and applied the brake, holding on while the sled settled on the ice and snow. As the dogs slowed their all-out run, Kat threw her snow hook into the snow.

When Sam's team formed a visual barrier in front of them, the lead dog on Al's team slowed to a stop.

Loki followed suit until both teams eased to a stop just short of Sam's.

Knees wobbling, Kat jumped from her runners and hurried to Al's side. Despite how creepy he'd been at the checkpoint in Nikolai, he was still a human being. An injured human who needed help.

When she reached his side, she yanked her goggles up and tugged a glove from her fingers. Then she knelt in the snow beside him, the frigid air biting her fingertips.

Frost and snow coated the man's scarf and his goggles had bounced loose, riding cockeyed over his nose. Kat unzipped his coat and shoved his woolen neck scarf aside to feel for the carotid artery. His skin was still warm but had already started cooling. After several attempts, Kat sat back.

The first signs of snow drifted down from the sky, sticking to Al's face instead of melting.

Sam joined her, kneeling on one knee beside her, his gaze panning the landscape. "We can't stay out in the open. No telling where our guy is."

Kat stared down at the dead man. "Who shot him? Who are we dealing with?"

"I'm not sure, but I have an idea." He glanced around again and then stood, pulling her to her feet.

"Then tell me. I need to understand what kind of sadistic bastard would kill like this."

"Not now, we have to keep moving." Sam urged her toward her sled.

Kat resisted, turning back toward Al Fendley. "We can't leave him here."

"He's dead."

"Still, we can't leave him."

Sam sighed. "All right, then help me load him onto my sled. We'll take him on to Takotna."

"We have to tell them what's going on. This isn't something we can keep from the officials and the media. All hell will break loose."

"Then we leave Al here and move on." Sam walked down Al's gangline, unhooking the dogs one at a time.

"What are you thinking?" Kat followed, freeing the dogs on the other side. "These dogs will show up in Takotna without a sled before us. How do we explain that?"

"We don't. I don't plan to go through Takotna. We're going around it and continuing on."

"That violates the race rules. The officials will get worried and send someone out."

"In case you hadn't noticed, this race is over for the two of us." After unhooking the lead dog, Sam straightened to his full height of over six feet tall. He strode across to Kat and stood toe-to-toe with her. "You should have stayed in McGrath. I didn't want you involved anymore."

"Tough. You had no right to leave without me." She pushed his chest with her open palms. "We're a team, remember? You rely on me, I rely on you. Got it?" She pushed him again.

Sam grabbed her hands and held them out in front of her. "We're not a team. I work alone. That's why I came to Alaska. I didn't want to work with anyone. So get that thought out of your head right now."

Her eyes narrowed. "Is that it? You had a partner and your partner sold out on you? What did he do, die like mine did?"

"No, it would have been better if he had." Sam dropped her hands and turned away.

Kat walked in front of him, forcing him to look at her. "Did you run away from the agency because your partner betrayed you?"

"Yes, damn it! He betrayed me by laundering money to terrorists."

At a loss for words, Kat could only stare at him.

"He got caught by the Saudi government, and I left him to rot in one of their prisons." He stared over her shoulder refusing to meet her gaze.

"It's not your fault he betrayed our country."

"A little girl died in the cross fire." He dropped his hands and moved away. "I should have seen what was happening before it got to that point. Look, the longer we stand out in the open, the better chance he has of shooting us, too." Sam strode across the snow to his sled, where he bent to check a bootie on one of his wheel dogs.

Kat followed him. "So you gave up because one man

betrayed you?" When he straightened, she moved closer. "You know, you're not as tough as I thought you were."

"What's that supposed to mean?" Sam's eyes narrowed.

"When the going gets tough, you leave."

"Think what you like." He moved to the side to go around her.

Kat positioned herself in front of him again. "Is it that you're afraid to trust anyone else or are you afraid to trust yourself?" The starch ran out of her words and they dropped into a soft whisper. "What is it, Sam?"

He closed his eyes, his jawline tightening until it looked as hard as stone. Then he grabbed her arms and shook her. "Why can't you leave it?" He shook her again.

Her teeth rattled and tears welled in her eyes. "Because, damn it, I care!"

For a long moment, he stared down into her eyes.

She cursed herself for the tears spilling over the edge and slipping down her cheeks. The moisture stung as the subzero air froze the liquid in place.

Sam pulled her hard against him.

Kat didn't protest, she let him hold her like she had wanted to be held since the race began.

When he lifted her chin with his gloved hand and smoothed the now-icy tears from her cheeks, she couldn't hold back. Her hands slid into the opening of his jacket and up beneath the scarf around his neck. She dragged him down until his lips hovered over hers. "Kiss me, damn it. You know you want to."

His mouth descended over hers and he kissed her. Long and hard, his tongue lashing out to scrape against her teeth until she opened her mouth to accept him. She sank deeper and deeper into him until she couldn't remember where she ended and Sam began.

Heat built inside her, pooling in the pit of her belly, spreading lower. She wanted more.

She could have stood there forever in the warmth and protection of Sam's arms.

The sharp crack of gunfire pulled them apart.

Chapter Twelve

Sam hit the snow before the second round went off, dragging Kat with him.

Al's dogs, loosened from their necklines, took off, following the grooves from previous mushers headed toward Takotna.

Kat dived low, the second shot pinging off a rock beside her foot.

Both remaining teams barked and jerked against their harness, eager to get the hell out of there.

"Run for it!" Sam yelled. He sprang to his feet and raced for his sled, already sliding across the ice.

Kat lunged for hers and pulled the snow hook up. "Let's go, go, go!" she shouted. Kat's team took the lead as Sam's swung in behind her.

More rounds exploded around them and then laughter rang in Sam's ears.

"Keep moving, Sam. You don't want me to get bored, do you?"

The man was playing with them again. Anger surged

through Sam. When the trail rounded a knoll, Sam stomped his brake and yelled, "Whoa!" He tossed out his snow hook.

Before the dogs came to a complete halt, Sam grabbed for his rifle and leaped off the runners.

Kat's team plowed ahead, unaware of Sam's sudden stop. She rounded another corner and disappeared.

Sam wanted her to keep going, but he couldn't stop what he was doing to tell her. Rifle in hand, he ran up the knoll, dropping low before he reached the crest.

As he crept to the top of the rise, the sound of an engine revving captured Sam's attention. A man on a snowmobile appeared out of the shadows along the top of a hill. He descended through the trees.

The snow fell faster now, the flakes fat, frozen crystals collecting on his goggles. Sam wiped his vision clear and aimed, patiently waiting for the man to clear the trees so that he could make his aim count. This might be his only chance to get him.

Just as Sam squeezed the trigger, a giant snowflake obscured his vision. When he wiped the goggles clean, the snowmobile had snaked around and disappeared over the top of a ridge.

"Damn!"

"Sam?" Kat's voice cut through Sam's disappointment and he rose from his position in the snow.

Switching his mic from Mute, he answered, "Yeah. Keep going, I'll catch you."

"You okay?"

"Yeah." And so was their BG, damn it.

Sam descended the hill and climbed on board his sled. "Let's go!" What he wouldn't give to have a snowmobile about now. He'd chase that son of a gun down.

The dogs were good, but they couldn't outrun the power of a snowmobile.

Kat must have slowed down considerably because within five minutes, he'd caught up to her, and a good thing he did.

The snow came down in force now and the wind had picked up, blowing at least thirty miles an hour.

"Don't forget to skirt Taktona, we'll go on to Ophir before we stop for the night," Sam said into the mic. He knew their BG was listening and he hoped he'd followed suit.

"Will do," was her terse response.

Sam switched his mic to Mute and pulled out the satellite phone.

Royce answered on the first ring. "Sam?"

"Yeah."

"Your killer shadow is Bradley English. Apparently, someone in our government made a deal with the Saudis to get him out a couple weeks ago."

"Who?"

"My sources said a senator from Alaska who knows about the S.O.S. and what they do."

"Blalock."

"He knows if Bradley kills you, the word won't get out. The government will do a cover-up to keep it quiet about the S.O.S. Which explains why he's on his way back. His hit man is out of control and he needs to make sure he doesn't do anything stupid, or spill the beans on his plan."

"Too late, he already did something stupid. He just killed a musher."

"Another man over the cliff?"

"No, this time he can't make it appear to be an accident. He shot Al Fendley in the back."

"I thought he was one of your suspects."

"I don't think many will miss him. The guy was a snake. However, when they find him, there will be a big hue and cry."

"That'll really bring the race to a halt, won't it?"

"Yes. I think we have a blizzard rolling in from the west, so they might not find him for another twenty-four hours or more."

Royce sighed. "In the meantime, you have to find Bradley and neutralize him before he gets away."

"Where are McNeal and Valdez?"

"Last I heard, they'd secured snowmobiles in Ruby and headed out to Cripple. They should be there by now."

"I hope they are. This weather is past ugly and bordering on deadly." He rang off and prayed the other two S.O.S. agents made it as far south as they could before the storm hit. If he wanted to catch Bradley, he'd need the help of other snowmobile operators trained in winter sniper operations.

SOON AFTER THEY bypassed Takotna, the weather turned even nastier. Kat could no longer see Sam's team behind her and the wind was making it difficult to keep her sled upright. Snow and drifts completely obliterated the trail. If not for the four-foot-high trail markers, they risked getting lost along the high ridge divide between the Kuskokwim and Innoko Rivers.

Sam had told her about ditching the GPS devices. If their BG wanted to keep up with them, he'd have to be following closely. Not that it made her feel any better. Before too much longer, they'd have to camp and ride out the storm.

Kat hoped their pursuer stopped, as well. He'd be a fool to try to attack them in a blizzard.

As she inched along at a snail's pace, darkness settled in with only the reflection of her sled's headlamp to guide them. When Kat could no longer see the trail markers on the right or left, she knew they had to seek shelter in the trees. Locating a copse of sturdy spruce, Kat pulled the team into the sheltered branches.

Sam pulled in beside her.

Doubled over in the wind, her clothing wet and cold, Kat moved methodically through the paces of setting out the remaining straw for each dog and attaching their individual blankets around their necks. She fed them and hoped they had enough to get them wherever they went next. Whether that would be Ophir or back to McGrath, Kat didn't know. All she knew was that she'd had enough running. Like Sam said, the race was over for them. Now, if they could just make it through this blizzard and convince one big bad guy of the same.

After Sam completed caring for his dogs, he cut away bows from the nearby spruce and lay them out for cush-

ioning between the snow and the tent he set up. He cut
more to help block the wind blowing over the dogs.

When he set out the tent, Kat helped him drive stakes
in the ground to keep the wind from blowing the ultra-
light fabric away before they could get inside.

By now the winds had to be blowing fifty miles an
hour with a windchill between minus forty and fifty
degrees. No matter how many layers of clothing she
wore, Kat couldn't get warm. Her teeth chattered so
hard her jaw ached. The wool scarf over her face had a
thick crust of ice and snow.

She bent low and crawled into the small tent as
quickly as she could to keep the snow flurries from following her in.

Sam moved in behind her, zipping shut the flap, trapping them in and the raging wind and snow out. With
both of them inside the tent, the tiny interior was even
smaller. Sam's broad shoulders seemed to stretch from
wall to wall. Kat couldn't move without bumping into
him. The beam from the flashlight only made the space
shrink further.

"Want some stew?" Sam opened the food bag and
emptied it on the floor of the tent.

"Sounds great." Feeling nervous and awkward, Kat
assembled and lit the cooker. Once the little flame
glowed, she extinguished the flashlight to save the
battery. She almost flicked it back on when she realized
how intimate and cozy the flame was.

Before long they'd consumed the stew and canned
crackers they'd brought.

The domed tent swayed in the gusts, but inside was semi-cozy, if not still cold.

Although the long silence had been comfortable, Kat wanted some answers. "Back on the trail you said you think you know this guy. Who is he?"

Sam stowed their dinner trash in a corner before he answered. "Remember when you'd guessed I'd failed a mission?"

"Yes."

He explained the Saudi assignment and resulting disaster, and told her about his most recent conversation with Royce.

"And you think this Bradley guy is the one after us?"

"Yes. I think Blalock brought him back to take care of me, knowing the government would wash it all under the rug, trying to keep the S.O.S. hush-hush."

"That's a lot of trouble to go through to kill one man."

"Not if you don't want anyone to know you've hired a killer to take out the one person holding your plans for road building and oil exploration in the interior."

"Why doesn't he just fire you and send in a geologist who'll find what he wants?"

"Blalock knows I'll take the information to Congress and stir up trouble. When he hired me, he never considered the oil might not be sufficient grade to tap into. He probably thought it was a slam dunk. With the troubles in the Middle East, all he had to do was find oil, and Congress would okay opening the territory to drilling."

"So what's in it for him?" Kat asked.

"There's money to be made, whether there's good oil out there or not. Building more roads to the interior can open an entirely new real-estate market, not to mention making it easier for the hunting outfitters to get their customers in, rather than always flying."

A chill racked Kat's body. "How can we get the goods on Blalock?"

Sam extinguished the cooker flame and switched on the flashlight. Immediately the temperature began to drop. "We have to get Bradley to talk."

Without the body-warming activity of guiding a sled and with the constant wind wailing outside flapping the fabric of the tent, Kat's body cooled. She snuggled down in her jacket, tucking her gloved fingers beneath her arms. "Then we need to be on the other end of the cat-and-mouse game."

"Agreed." Sam pulled off a glove and unzipped his sleeping bag. As he spread the flaps open, his shoulders bumped into her with each movement.

How could Kat remain unaware of the man in these close confines? "What's our plan?"

He stilled and cast a glance her way. "We need to set a trap to catch our mouse."

"And for bait?" The cold knot of fear in Kat's belly gave her the answer before Sam voiced it.

"Me." As if emphasizing his point, he shook his sleeping bag open.

"Isn't there another way? Can't we call in the Coast Guard or someone to conduct an aerial search for him?"

"No. He'll expose the S.O.S. and completely blow

the organization wide-open. We have to capture him and put him away, someplace he can't make a noise."

"But to use you as bait?" She shook her head. There had to be another way.

"He wants me." Sam shrugged. "Why not give him what he wants?"

Kat's brow settled into a frown. "That doesn't sound like such a good plan to me." But for the life of her, she couldn't come up with a better one.

"It's all about timing. As soon as this storm passes, Valdez and McNeal should get here within a couple hours."

"It only takes a second for a bullet to kill a man," she pointed out.

"Have faith." He smiled and tipped her chin up. "Have I let you down yet?"

"No, but—" His touch sent warm tremors throughout her body, chasing away the cold seeping into her fingers and toes. When he dropped his hand, she wished for it back.

"No buts. We're going to do this."

"Where do I come in?" She grabbed his hand and stared into his eyes. "And don't think you're going to leave me behind again."

His fingers curled around hers. "You'll be the ace up my sleeve. I'll have you to shoot him if he tries to kill me before the troops arrive."

"And he won't know I'm there, how?" Kat liked the way his hand felt against hers and she wondered what it would feel like spread out across her body.

He pulled her closer and whispered against her ear. "We'll fake your death."

"Fake my death?" Another chill shook her entire body with enough force to rattle her teeth.

"I think a sled crash." Sam frowned and leaned back. "You're getting cold, aren't you?"

"A little." She pushed aside his concern, more interested in this plan than her comfort. "So, I'm supposed to play dead and wait for him to do what…shoot you?"

Sam grinned. "Something like that."

The grin threw her into a tailspin and Kat fought to keep the plan germinating. He looked like a kid about to pull a silly prank instead of a man going up against a killer who'd already shot one man and pushed another off a cliff. Another shiver shook her body.

"You're shaking." Sam glanced around the tent. "We need to settle in for the storm. It's only going to get colder." He reached out and felt her jacket and snow pants. "These are wet."

"Yeah, and so are yours. We should shed our outer clothes so they can dry."

"I have a better idea, why don't we zip our bags together and share body warmth?" When Kat didn't move, Sam continued, "I promise not to bite. It makes sense, unless you plan to freeze in your cold wet jacket."

Sleep inside a bag with Sam? What was her problem? With the temperature dipping by the hour, she'd be shaking all night if she didn't take him up on the offer.

Sam grabbed her sleeping bag, zipping the ends to his. Before she could come up with any excuses, Kat shed her jacket and snow pants and hopped into the bag. Sam shed his outer garments and joined her.

Kat's body trembled all over, not as much from cold as from anticipation, and now the reality of being this close to Sam. If she didn't plan on both of them freezing, then she'd better get a whole lot closer.

She slid closer to Sam and wrapped her arms around his waist. "They say you can avoid hypothermia by sharing body warmth."

His arms encircled her and he brought her closer. "I've heard that, but never had to put it to the test."

"Well, now's our chance to test the theory." With her nose pressed to his chest, she could hardly think past the fresh clean scent of snow, wool and aftershave. "Are you getting warmer?"

"Oh, yeah." The tip of his chin rubbed against her forehead. His two-days' worth of stubble rasping against her skin set her nerves on alert.

She could get used to being held in Sam's arms, like the other night when she'd had the bad dream. He'd been there to hold her, asking for nothing in return.

Only this time was different. This time she was wide awake, and for the past several days she hadn't thought much about Marty at all. She'd spent a lot of time thinking about Sam, admiring his work with the dogs, the way his broad shoulders looked even broader in his parka and snow gear.

Now she was lying next to him, the warmth of his breath stirring tendrils of hair across her forehead.

"I can't believe I'm doing this," she murmured, suddenly less afraid and more empowered by the intensity of her longing. She wanted to be held, to be touched. Not just by any man, but by this one. She'd agreed to the race, not to win, but to keep Sam safe. After days on the trail, suffering many of the same hardships, being shot at and nearly killed, she found that being with Sam had made her feel more alive than she'd felt in a year.

Instead of her saving him, he'd saved her from dying a slow and painful death inside. He'd shown her there was life after Marty. Just because he'd died didn't mean she had to die, as well.

Sam's hands kneaded into her lower back, the spot that ached from standing all day.

Kat moaned. "Mmm, that feels good." Her fingers gripped the front of Sam's sweater. "When this is all over, you'll be out of a job."

"I know."

"What's next?" Was that her breathy voice? Had she been concentrating too hard on what his hands were doing she forgot what they were talking about? While he massaged her back, he brought forth her own need to touch, to stroke. Beneath her fingertips, his chest was solid, firm and muscular. She wondered how it would feel to press her hands to his skin.

"You tell me."

Tell him what? Her brain had fogged with pure sensation. "Right there. You could become a masseur. You're hands are magical." She sighed, her muscles relaxing, her cheek resting against his arm.

"Like that, huh?"

Was that his lips touching her forehead?

Kat tipped her head back and Sam's lips captured hers. Heat suffused her entire body, pooling low in her belly. After their last kiss, she didn't know what to expect. Had it only been a reaction to the circumstances?

The kiss inspired a hunger so deep and so ravenous, she couldn't stop her hands from skimming over his chest and down to the hem of his shirt. She had to feel him, touch him, even if just for a moment. When her fingers touched his warm skin, she couldn't stop there. What she felt, she had to see.

"Do you know what you're doing to me?" He pressed a kiss to her jaw and nuzzled her earlobe.

"If it's half what you're doing to me, we're in trouble." She shoved his shirt up and slid down his body to plant a kiss on his tight abs. With her cheek pressed against his belly, the hard ridge of his trousers pressed into the valley between her breasts. Warmth spread lower to the juncture of her thighs and Kat's breath caught in her throat in a rush of longing and the ache of desire she hadn't experienced in over a year.

Sam's fingers smoothed over her hair and down to sweep against the sides of her breasts. "Come here." He pulled her up to take her lips again, rolling her over on the sleeping bag until his body pinned her beneath him.

"Wouldn't this whole sharing warmth thing work better naked?" She couldn't slow the momentum.

With hands trembling from need, she pushed his sweater up and over his head. Frustrated by the layers, she grabbed the turtleneck and long-john shirts and pushed them both up and over his head. Finally, she reached the steely strength of his chest encased in taut, tanned skin and sprinkled with a healthy smattering of light blond, crisp curls.

She drank in what she could see from the beam of the single flashlight she'd tucked inside the sleeping bag with them.

His skin glowed bronze, the dark brown nipples puckered in the freezing night air. "It's cold in here. Want to zip this bag up the rest of the way?"

"Mmm…yes. But first…" She struggled beneath him, reaching for her own sweater, pulling it up over her head and shoving it to the bottom of the sleeping bag.

"Need some help?" He grasped the bottom of her turtleneck and insulated-underwear top and dragged them slowly up her body until he'd removed all but her less-than-sexy pink cotton bra. Not that it mattered when she reached beneath her and unclasped the hooks, shrugging out of the straps. "Now! Close the bag now!"

Sam hesitated for a moment, his warm gaze roving over the effect the cold was having on Kat's skin.

Gooseflesh sprang up and the tips of her nipples hardened into tight buds. As the same cold penetrated his awareness and raised similar gooseflesh on his skin, he grabbed for the zipper and ran it the rest of the way around until they were cocooned inside the double sleeping bag.

Kat shivered, the cold having returned some of her brain cells to functioning order. She'd half stripped in front of a stranger. How long had she really known

Sam? A week, tops? Had she gone completely out of her mind? As soon as he quit fiddling with the zipper, he leaned over her and brushed a strand of hair across her cheek. "Are you sure about this?"

Was he out of his mind to give her an out now? What man asked such a question when a woman had practically stripped him?

A man like Sam.

A man who cared more about others than his own physical discomfort. A man who put his dogs' needs ahead of his own. A man who'd been betrayed by his partner and absorbed the mission failure as his own. What was not to love about him?

Love? Kat's breath stuttered in her chest. Was she ready to love again? After loving Marty so much she'd almost died with his death, was she ready to love Sam and expose herself to further heartache? She didn't know if she could survive another loss so great.

With his ex-partner determined to kill him, Sam wasn't a good risk. But she wanted him. Now. Could she just slake her sexual thirst and walk away unscathed? Dare she?

Sam leaned back. "We don't have to do this." He touched her lips in a brief but gentle kiss, then leaned up on his arms. "Just say no, and we'll call it off."

She couldn't have said no if she'd wanted to. Her body took over, screaming from every nerve cell to take what he offered. Kat's hands circled his neck and pulled him closer until her lips hovered beneath his. "Please. Warm me up."

His naked chest skimmed across her breasts. Rather

than crush her with his weight, he rolled to his side and pulled her into his arms. Despite the tightness of his jeans pressing into her belly, he held back. He rested his forehead against hers and kissed the tip of her nose. "What am I going to do with you?"

"How about the obvious?" She wasn't hesitant in the least. Once she'd made up her mind, she went after what she wanted. Her hands skimmed over his shoulders and down his back. With her breasts pressed firmly against his chest, she circled them in the springy curls, loving the slight abrasive quality, tantalizing her and sending ripples of sensations coursing south.

Sam's fingers dug into her hair, tugging her head back until he could claim her lips in a soul-defining kiss that rocked her to her core. Tugging harder, he tipped her head back, exposing the long line of her neck. There, he placed tiny kisses, alternating with flicks of his warm wet tongue and tender nibbles.

Kat wanted more, guiding him downward until the rough bristles of his chin skimmed across her nipples. Breath refused to move in and out of her lungs as she hung suspended, awaiting the touch of his tongue on her breast.

When he obliged, the breath she'd held exhaled in a moan, her back arching to press her nipple deeper into his mouth.

He sucked on the tip, laving the hardened bead with his tongue before transferring his attention to the other equally sensitive breast.

The wind slammed against the outside of the tent, matching the force of sensations raging through Kat's body. With each touch, she gasped, the apex of her thighs growing hot and moist.

Sam nudged her legs apart with his knee, rubbing his thigh against her center.

Kat's fingers dug into his back, pushing him lower until he skimmed her belly with his tongue, driving downward until he reached the waistband of her sweats. Inch by inch, he slid the elastic down her hips, lapping a trail of tongue flicks until he reached the top of her pink bikini panties.

No longer content to take it slow, Kat shimmied the rest of the way out of her sweats and long underwear.

Sam hooked a finger beneath the elastic of her panties, but he didn't drag them down as Kat longed for him to do. He slid inside and touched her there, at that hot, wet center.

Kat arched off the floor of the tent, her hand pressing his against her, pushing his finger deeper.

A long low moan sounded outside the tent, the wind forcing its way through the bows of the spruce trees. Kat matched the wind moan for moan as Sam pushed more fingers inside her then dragged her juices up to stroke that most sensitive of places.

Her arousal rocketed with the fury of the storm, shooting up in a crescendo of heat and desire. "Please, come to me now!" she gasped.

Sam jerked his jeans off and stripped her panties down past her ankles. Then he settled between her legs, the tip of his erection pressing into her wetness.

Kat wrapped her legs around his waist and brought him home in one tight jerk of her calves.

As she exploded over the edge, a cacophony of impulses blitzed throughout her body, setting every nerve ending on fire.

Sam rocked in and out of her until he jerked to a halt, his breathing suspended as he held her hips tightly against his, his manhood buried deep inside. Then he yanked free of her before he spilled his juices.

Shocked by his consideration and by the cooler air touching where he'd been, Kat lay still against the soft fabric of the sleeping bag. The flannel against her naked backside rubbed deliciously against her skin, making her feel wicked, wanton and completely satisfied.

Sam collapsed beside her and eased her into his arms. He rested his chin against the top of her head, his breathing still erratic, rasping in and out of his chest.

Kat's own pulse began to slow and a cozy warmth filled her insides. She snuggled closer, loving the feel of his skin next to hers. The connection between their bodies acted like a furnace, warming them against the cold threatening to penetrate the tent and the sleeping bag.

"What am I going to do with you?" Sam repeated his earlier question.

"When you catch your breath, you can do what you just did again."

His arms tightened around her and he laughed, the deep tone rumbling through his chest into hers. "Already? Aren't you the least bit tired?"

After all the time on the trail, all the worry and strain, Kat should have been exhausted. "Sure, I'm tired, but I think I could find a little more energy."

"Yeah. I think you could." His knee slipped between hers.

"How cold do you think it is out there?" she asked, pressing a kiss to his neck.

Sam bent to nibble her ear. "Damn cold."

"Do you think the dogs are okay?"

"Yeah. I covered them with branches. That'll create a cave in the snow to block the wind."

"Thanks." She scooted closer, resting her hands against his chest. "About tomorrow."

He kissed her nose and then pressed another kiss to her lips, running his tongue along the seam until she opened her mouth, accepting him inside. When he finally came up for air, he asked, "What about tomorrow?"

Kat's hand slid around his waist and down to rest on the hard muscle of his buttock. She pulled him forward until his member pressed into her belly. Burying her face in his neck, she whispered, "I'm scared."

Chapter Thirteen

After caring for the dogs, Sam removed the satellite phone from his pocket.

"Hey, that's mine." Kat frowned. "Are you ever going to give it back?"

"After I find out where Valdez and McNeal are." He dialed in to the number Royce gave him the night before. After the tenth ring, a voice answered.

"Yeah?"

"Valdez or McNeal?" Sam asked.

"It's McNeal. Valdez is with me."

"Hey, Sean, good to hear your voice."

"Same to you, Sam. Proves you're still alive." McNeal laughed. "Not that Bradley can bring you down. You always were a better agent than him. When are you coming back to work?"

"About the same time you settle down and get married."

A snort sounded in Sam's ear, followed by McNeal's statement. "Did that. Got married six months ago."

"No kidding? The world's most confirmed bachelor

got married?" He stared across at Kat, who mouthed "McNeal?" He nodded.

So much time had passed and he hadn't kept in touch. Now he wished he had. Until he heard McNeal's voice, he hadn't realized how much he missed his friends at the agency.

Sean McNeal laughed. "So when are you comin' back?"

After a deep breath, Sam said in a quiet voice. "Got a problem to fix today."

"So I hear." Leaving the jokes behind, McNeal's voice was all business. "We had to hunker down in Cripple last night during the storm. We hit the trail over an hour ago and should be in Ophir in less than forty-five minutes."

"By my calculations, we're about twelve miles southeast of Ophir. We're staying pretty close to the trail, but we're about to set a trap for English."

"Frankly, I'm surprised the traitor is still alive."

"You and me both. Now we have to catch him. My guess is you're about an hour away from us. That gives me an hour to put our plan in place."

"Should have figured you had a plan. Fill me in."

While Sam filled Sean in on the plan to lure Bradley out, Kat checked her lines, fitting the dogs with fresh booties before they started out on their dangerous mission.

She moved with quiet confidence, as if her last words to Sam last night had never been spoken. This tough woman who could mush the most dangerous trails through the harsh Alaskan landscape and fight her way out of missions gone bad as an S.O.S. agent had admitted to being scared.

Somehow that, more than anything, started Sam's day out on the wrong foot. To be truthful, he wasn't feeling very sure of himself, either. If his timing was off and all hell broke loose, both he and Kat could die and Bradley English would, once again, get away with murder.

Sam couldn't let that happen. Bradley had to be stopped. But at what cost? He couldn't let anything happen to Kat. In the past few days, she'd reminded him of why he had loved working with the S.O.S. Helping to ensure a better country and defend the greater good, not just himself, had made him feel as if he was contributing.

There were good people who needed the backing and support of the S.O.S. If Bradley ran free, no telling what would happen. He might expose the whole group, possibly placing the agents on current undercover missions in serious danger.

Bradley had to be stopped.

Sam hoped that by having Kat fake her death she'd be out of Bradley's crosshairs long enough for Sam to confront him and take him down.

He'd set up a code word for Kat when they found a defendable and logical place in the trail to have her "accident." First, he needed to know Bradley was still following them after the blizzard last night. Without the GPS tracking device, Bradley had to have stayed close.

The sound of a snowmobile engine echoed off the hillsides.

"Come on. I want to be closer to McNeal and Valdez before we initiate Operation Dead Dog Down."

"Tell me that's not what you're calling it." Kat rolled her eyes. "I believe my dogs are offended."

Sam smiled.

He strode across the snow, pulled her into his arms and crushed her lips with his own. "Don't get smart with me."

"Never. Can't show you up, it might injure your delicate ego." Her lips twisted in an attempt to keep a smile from spreading across her face. Then the twinkle died from her eyes. "Take care, will you?"

"Same to you." He stared hard into her eyes. "When this is over, we need to talk."

"About last night—"

Sam shook his head. "Not now. Later."

"But—"

He touched a gloved finger to her lips. "Later."

Kat took the lead, Sam preferring to keep her in his sights at all times.

"Let's go!" Kat shouted.

The team leaped, straining against their harnesses, gaining a sluggish start in the newly fallen six inches of snow. Kat ran along behind the sled then pedaled with one foot until they were whisking through the powder, edging back toward the trail markers.

With every intention of giving Bradley their location and current movements, Sam left his mic on. "We're about fifteen miles from Ophir. We'll have to stop there to pick up food for the dogs."

"Roger," Kat responded.

Sam remained alert to every sound outside the swish of sled runners on snow and the occasional dog barking. When the distinct sound of a snowmobile engine penetrated the wool flaps covering his ears, he knew his bogey had caught up.

Ahead, the trail bypassed a bridge, dropping down into one of the creeks that flowed into the Innoko River. This was as good a place as any, with cover and concealment for Kat and rough terrain sufficient to capsize a sled.

Sam gave Kat the signal, "Doing okay up there?"

Kat responded with the key phrase indicating she'd received his cue to tip her sled. "As well as to be expected."

From this point forward, Operation Dead Dog Down was under way. Anything could happen.

Sam sent up a silent prayer as Kat dipped down into the creek. Her sled jolted and bounced. Instead of balancing on one runner to keep from tipping over, she toppled onto her side. The sled continued to slide forward on the uneven, icy ground, dragging her along with it. With the sled on its side and too unwieldy to pull out of the creek bed, the dogs stopped.

"Kat?" Sam called into his headset. "Kat?" When she didn't respond, blood pounded against Sam's ears. He slammed on his brake and threw out the snow hook, stopping his team at the top of the trail leading down into the creek. Striker peered down at Kat's team, barking and wagging his tail.

Several of Kat's team barked in response.

Sam raced to the edge of the creek and stared down at her. "Kat? Kat, are you all right?"

She didn't move or say a word, lying as still as death, her eyes closed.

"Kat?" Sam slid down the creek bank and dropped to his knees on the hard-packed snow and ice. "Kat, answer me." He lifted her head, pushing aside her goggles. "Kat, sweetheart, wake up." Sam squeezed her hand, then bent to press a light kiss to her lips. "It's going to be okay, Kat, really it is. We have to get you to Ophir. They'll know what to do. Kat, please wake up."

"Having difficulties, Russell?" Bradley's voice sounded in Sam's earphones.

"Kat's hurt." Sam spoke into his mic. "I have to get her to a doctor."

Bradley snorted. "You're not getting her anywhere."

"What do you mean? If I don't get her someplace soon, she could die. She's unconscious, do you hear me?" Sam's voice rose, his desperation echoed in every word.

"So what?" An engine revved at the top of the opposite creek bank and settled into idle. "I could care less whether or not the bitch dies."

Anger swelled inside Sam as he glanced up at the man who'd betrayed his own country. "I'm taking her to Ophir." He stood, facing his former partner.

Bradley climbed from his snowmobile, yanked his goggles off at the same time as he pulled what looked like a SIG pistol from his pocket. "Don't move."

Without the static of the headset, the man's voice was familiar and his face even more so.

"Get out of my way, English," Sam said, his voice firm, unbending. He stood with his legs in a ready stance, wishing he could reach the pistol in his pocket before Bradley could fire his weapon. "She needs help."

"If you don't want me to shoot her now, you'll get on your sled, Sam." Bradley shot into the snow at Sam's feet. "Do it!"

Sam cast a glance down at Kat, his frown deepening. He didn't want to leave her exposed to the elements. "Just leave her out of this. Your beef is with me."

"Damn right it is. You left me in that hellhole to rot."

"You killed a child and got caught."

"She was collateral damage."

"She didn't have to be. If you hadn't been negotiating weapons sales to Saudi terrorists, she wouldn't be dead."

"If you had stayed out of it, she wouldn't have gotten caught in the middle." He jerked his hand to the side. "Leave her, you're coming with me."

When Sam hesitated, Bradley shifted his aim to Kat. "You'll come with me now or I'll shoot you both. It's your choice."

Sam's hand dropped toward his pocket.

Bradley aimed at Sam's chest. "I suggest you toss your weapon on the ground right now."

When Sam didn't move, Bradley aimed to the side of Kat's head and fired off a round.

She didn't even flinch when snow and dirt bounced up in her face.

"Okay, okay. Don't shoot her." Sam reached into his pocket and pulled out his pistol, swinging his hand like he would toss it, only he gripped it harder and pulled the trigger.

Bradley's weapon exploded.

Fire erupted in Sam's shoulder and the force of Bradley's bullet spun him around and away from the woman lying on the ground.

Kat rolled onto her belly behind the sled, slamming the butt of her rifle into her shoulder. Just as she aimed and squeezed the trigger, something hit the side of her head so hard, she jerked back and her shot went wide.

Kat fell back, a red stain spilling out onto the virgin-white snow.

Clutching his injured arm, Sam dropped to the ground next to Kat. She'd been hit in the side of the head. With his good hand, he pushed her parka hood and hat to the side and stared down at the blood oozing from the wound. "Kat!"

No response.

Another round exploded next to him and Sam jumped to his feet. "Bastard!"

"On your sled, now, or I shoot her again."

"I can't leave her like this." His breath came in shallow gasps, pain searing through his shoulder, an even greater pain burning in his heart at the sight of Kat lying so still.

"You will or she'll die anyway." Bradley fired another round, this time hitting beside her ear, tearing into the parka hood.

"Okay, okay, stop shooting and I'll go with you." Sam's chest squeezed in a tight knot. How could he leave her like this? Before, it had all been part of their plan. Not now. Kat didn't wake when he'd called out her name, and Bradley didn't give Sam time to check for a pulse.

Sam straightened, the weight of his mistakes pulling at his feet as he climbed the creek bank to his sled. His right arm hung limp at his side. Left-handed, he'd be useless in hand-to-hand combat with Bradley. All he could hope was to get Bradley away from Kat so he couldn't inflict further injury on her. If she lived, Valdez and McNeal would find her soon and get her back to safety.

Sam had to believe that. Kat couldn't die for his mistaken planning.

Climbing on his sled, Sam pulled up the snow hook and clung to the handlebar with his left hand. "Let's go!"

Bradley waved his pistol. "You take the lead. I'll tell you when to turn off the trail."

It took every ounce of willpower to pass Kat lying in the snow at the bottom of the creek, possibly dying. Her face was pale, her dark eyelashes fanned out on her cheeks. She resembled a sleeping angel.

Her dogs yelped and lunged at their harnesses, eager to get moving again.

Sam called out to them. "Stay!"

If Kat came to, she'd need her sled to get her to Ophir. From there they'd get her back to Anchorage and a hospital.

As the distance widened between Bradley and Kat, Sam's mind raced. He had to do something to overpower Bradley. But what?

A mile down the road from the creek, Bradley spoke into the headset. "Turn right."

Sam followed some fresh snowmobile tracks. Soon an old cabin appeared, nestled among spruce trees. This must be where Bradley stayed through the blizzard. Ahead of them on the trail to make sure he didn't miss them passing through.

"We stop here."

"Whoa!" Sam yelled, stomping his foot brake. When the sled slid to a stop, he stepped from the runners and set out the snow hook. His head spun with each movement. His shoulder wound had begun to ache with fierce intensity. When he straightened his arm, blood dripped from the bottom of his sleeve.

Bradley climbed off his snowmobile, the pistol still in his hand, his gloved finger taking up all the space in the trigger. Wouldn't take much for him to fire another round.

Sam swayed, fighting back waves of gray. "What do you want with me?"

"I want you inside."

"No, we handle this here, now."

Bradley shot at the ground in front of Sam. "Inside."

"No."

His eyes narrowing to slits, Bradley aimed at Sam's lead dog, Striker. "Inside or the dog dies."

Sam ground his teeth together. Bradley had his number. Threaten those around him, including the dogs, and he'd get him to do anything. Once inside, there wasn't anything else Bradley could threaten to shoot but him. Sam pushed the door open and stepped inside.

Bradley stepped in behind him, pressing the pistol into the base of Sam's spine. Once they'd cleared the doorway, Bradley shoved Sam hard.

The momentum sent him sailing across the small room, stumbling over broken furniture and a stack of firewood. He hit the wall on the far side of the room with the wounded shoulder. Pain shot through his arm like a battalion of razor blades. Sam sank to his knees, fighting waves of nausea and darkness.

Bradley stood over him. "Do you know what they do to prisoners in Saudi prisons?"

Sam rocked back on his heels, struggling to remain conscious. He had to neutralize Bradley and get back to Kat.

"Let me give you a sample." Bradley kicked him in the stomach.

Sam doubled over, his forehead hitting the hard wood slats of the ancient floor. Another kick hit him in the side of the head and Sam slammed up against the wall. He knew if he stayed down, Bradley would finish him off. When Bradley's foot flew at him again, Sam dodged the blow and grabbed his ankle with his good hand.

Using Bradley's momentum, he spun him around and shoved hard.

The gun went off, firing into the thick wood logs. Bradley flung out his hands to keep from slamming face-first into the wall. He lost his grip on the gun and it dropped to the floor, skidding toward the open door.

Sam stood, the effort making his head swim.

When Bradley dived for the gun, Sam launched all his weight toward him, hitting him hard in the back of the knees. Together, they crashed to the floor.

Pain racked Sam's arm and although he fought to stay alert, darkness crept in around him.

Bradley inched his way out from under Sam's body and reached for the gun.

The room went black.

KAT CAME TO with a dog licking her face and whining. When she opened her eyes, Loki's black-and-white face and blue eyes hovered over her.

He whined again, his tail wagging slowly.

"Loki?"

The dog yelped, his tail sweeping the air in wide, urgent arcs.

When she glanced around, the white glare of freshly fallen snow blinded her, sending achy twinges into her right temple. Her hand rose to press against the offending temple only to cause a more excruciatingly sharp pain to shoot through her head, blurring her vision.

She glanced at her gloved hand. It was covered in blood. Her blood. Dizziness assailed her and she squeezed her eyes shut for a moment to keep the trees from spinning around in circles.

The roar of snowmobiles penetrated her brain and her eyes opened in time to see two machines top the creek banks above her and dive down to where she lay.

Dogs erupted in yelps and howling.

Still in a fog, Kat patted the snow beside her for something to defend herself with. Her hand landed on her rifle and she sat up, pressing the butt of the weapon against her shoulder. "Stop right there or I'll shoot!" Bright lights flashed in her head and she swayed, the rifle dropping to the ground beside her. *Oh, crud. Don't do it. Don't pass out again.* She swayed and fell back, her head smacking against the hard-packed snow.

"Kat?" The first man off the machine reached her side and called out, "Kat!"

"McNeal?" She rubbed a hand over her eyes and stared up into Sean McNeal's dark eyes. "Damn, you're a sight for sore eyes."

"You're just a sight." He pushed aside her hair and winced.

"Looks bad, but it's just a flesh wound." Kat grabbed his arm. "Mind giving me a hand up?"

"I think you should stay down." McNeal pressed her shoulders back against the ground. "Where's Sam?"

"That's why I want up." She pushed his hands away from her shoulders and struggled to sit, determined to stay upright this time. She stared around at the tracks marring the snow deposited by the previous night's storm. "Looks like Sam left with Bradley. You didn't see anyone between Ophir and here?"

"Only one musher." McNeal shook his head. "Not Russell."

McNeal stood and held out his hand. "I suppose there's no use trying to convince you to stay here while we go after him, is there?"

"None." She accepted the extended hand and McNeal pulled her to her feet, wrapping an arm around her waist when she swayed. "I'll be all right, it's Sam I'm worried about." She glanced across at Valdez. "Hey, got room on the back of that machine for me?"

Casanova Valdez's brows wrinkled. "Yeah, if you

Alaskan Fantasy

promise not to fall off. You look like one of Freddy Krueger's victims."

"Thanks." Rifle in hand, Kat staggered across the snow to McNeal's snowmobile, instead. "It's good to see you, too, Cass. If it's all right by you, I'll ride with McNeal. I've seen the way you drive."

McNeal swung his leg over the seat and scooted up to allow room for Kat.

Her head splitting in two, Kat held on to McNeal's shoulder with her empty hand and slid her leg across the seat, settling in behind him. "You probably passed them on the way here. Bradley might have directed him off trail. Let's go, we should be able to find their tracks."

"You sure you're up to holding on?"

"Damn right. Sam needs me…us." The truth was she needed Sam. After the past few days on the trail, Kat realized how much she needed him in her life. For the past year, she'd floundered. Sure, she missed Marty, but he was dead. Sam had reawakened feelings she'd thought dead with Marty and, damn it, she wanted more. She refused to let Bradley English take her last chance at happiness away from her, especially when she hadn't had the opportunity to fully explore it.

The dogs barked and yelped, confused at being left behind. Kat couldn't help that. She'd be back soon to collect them and get them back to Anchorage. First, Sam had to be found and rescued from that psychotic ex-agent.

Every bump sent shards of pain slicing through her brain, but Kat held on and watched for signs of one sled team and one snowmobile leaving the trail. A couple miles past the creek, Kat saw it. Thank God for last night's blizzard. The tracks in the fresh snow could be none other than Sam and Bradley.

"Stop!" Kat banged her rifle against McNeal's shoulder to get his attention. "Cut the engine."

Even before McNeal switched the engine off, Kat was off the machine and giving Valdez the slicing motion across her throat.

He, too, killed his engine and hopped off the snowmobile, pulling a pistol from his pocket.

Armed with her rifle, Kat followed the tracks through the snow at a slow jog, McNeal and Valdez beside her. How far off the danged trail were they? She'd begun to think she'd made a mistake, when the trees opened into a small clearing where a derelict cabin nestled against the spruce trees. The sound of a scuffle drifted through the open doorway.

Scuffling was good. Scuffling took two people, which meant Sam was alive. A rush of hope spurred Kat on and she sprinted toward the shelter.

Before they reached the building, Bradley English landed on his belly in the doorway.

Sam sprawled across his legs like a profootball linebacker.

Before McNeal, Valdez or Kat could reach the man, Bradley grabbed a gun and pointed it at Kat.

"Make one more move, and I'll shoot her," Bradley gasped.

Sam wasn't moving. But then Kat noticed the blood smeared across his shoulder and Bradley's leg. No, Sam wasn't going anywhere. He'd done all he could do. It was up to the rest of them to deal with Bradley.

After all the heartache he'd caused, Kat wasn't willing to cut the guy any slack.

"Put your weapons on the ground, now!" Bradley yelled. The man's legs were trapped beneath Sam's torso. He'd have trouble climbing out from under him.

If Kat played her cards right. "You might as well give it up, Bradley. The game's over." She inched forward a step.

"Stop where you are and drop your rifle." He balanced his pistol in his palm, aiming it at Kat's chest, while struggling to free his legs.

Just another foot and she'd be in position.

"I said drop it!" Bradley's hand shook and he finally freed his legs.

Kat darted forward and kicked as hard as she could. Her toe connected with Bradley's wrist as the gun exploded.

The shot went wild, whizzing past Kat's head and disappearing into the snow. The pistol flew from Bradley's hands and bounced against the wall.

The man pushed to his feet and lurched toward Kat, his hands outstretched, anger giving his face a mottled red-and-purple hue.

Valdez fired, clipping the man in the left shoulder.

Bradley jerked off course for a moment. With his face set in a livid mask, he rushed at Kat again.

McNeal plugged the man in the chest with another bullet.

Bradley staggered backward, his eyes wide, blood

gurgling in his throat. Then he dropped to his knees and fell face-first in the snow.

Though Kat felt as if she could fall to the snow, as well, she hurried to Sam's side and tried to roll him over. He was like a dead weight. "Help me turn him over!" she shouted, her eyes pooling, blinding her.

McNeal and Valdez appeared beside her and rolled Sam to his back.

He'd been hit in the shoulder, and by the looks of it had lost a lot of blood.

Kat stripped off her jacket and her sweater. Next she pulled her soft cotton turtleneck over her head and wadded it up. The cold hit her like a Mack truck. She ignored it, unzipping and pushing aside Sam's jacket to reveal the wound in his shoulder.

McNeal spoke into a satellite phone behind her, "Tazer, get a hold of the Alaska Air folks and have a helicopter flown in to these coordinates." He read off a string of coordinates from the GPS device he held in his other hand. "Tell them to hurry. We have two people down."

"Come on, Sam, you can't leave me now. We have a race to finish." Kat pressed the soft cotton shirt to the wound, applying pressure to stop the bleeding. How much blood had he lost? She touched a hand to his face.

His skin was pale and cool.

"We need a fire in here," she said, her teeth beginning to chatter. "Please."

Valdez gathered firewood and shoved it into the ancient potbellied stove in the corner of the cabin. After several minutes he had a nice fire burning and he brought in Sam's sleeping bag.

Together, Kat and McNeal rolled Sam into the bag and zipped it.

"Is he going to make it?" Kat asked, unable to hold back tears any longer. "Oh God, please tell me he'll make it." Her shoulders shook and she lay her head across Sam's chest.

"You took my advice." A soft whisper penetrated Kat's sobs.

"Sam?" Kat leaned back, brushing the tears from her eyes.

He stared up at her, his eyelids drooping but open. "We got him, didn't we?"

"Yes, we did."

"Couldn't have done it without my partner."

"No, you couldn't." She lifted his hand to her wet cheek. "We're a team now."

"Damn right we are." He touched a finger to a fat tear rolling down her face. "It's okay to cry."

"I know," she said. "I know."

Chapter Fourteen

Paul hobbled through the living room, still sporting his ankle brace but having given up the crutches. "Hurry up, they're here!"

Kat lit the last candle and stood back to admire her handiwork. She'd never been one for decorating or cooking, but staring around the house festooned in candles, sparkle lights and with the table filled to over-flowing with food, she could almost feel the ache in her arm from patting herself on the back.

"You wearing that?" Paul frowned at her black slacks and black V-neck sweater. "You'd think you could wear a skirt just this once. If you want to impress a guy, you have to show a little leg."

"And who says I'm trying to impress anyone?" She turned away before her brother could see the color rise in her heated cheeks.

Paul snorted and grabbed for the door handle just as the doorbell rang.

Kat glanced down at her pants and shirt. What was

wrong with the clothes she had on? For a mad, crazy moment, she debated making a dash for her room to change into a bright red miniskirt. Then she remembered she didn't even own a miniskirt. What you see is what you get. After all, she really wasn't trying to impress anyone.

Then why is your gut in a knot and why are your palms sweating?

Her breath lodged in her throat as the door swung open.

Tazer stepped through. "Hi, sweetie." She pecked Paul with a kiss on the cheek. "Miss me?"

"You bet." He wrapped a brotherly arm around her and squeezed. "Kat's been dying to see you."

She glanced across the room, a smile curving her lips. "I'll bet she's glad to see someone, and I bet that someone isn't me." With a graceful turn, she looked behind her. "Are you coming in or not?"

Then he was there, standing in the entrance, his shoulders blocking the light from the afternoon sun.

Sam.

With the backlight behind him, his face was cast in shadows, making his expression unreadable. The man had been gone for nearly a month. Kat had only seen him for a few minutes in the hospital in Anchorage before they flew him to Bethesda, Maryland, for surgery and the beginning of his physical-therapy sessions. He'd spent two weeks in the hospital and two additional weeks of therapy, during which he traveled to D.C. to present his findings.

While he'd been gone, he hadn't called or written to her, not a letter, e-mail, nothing.

She should be angry with him. After all they'd been through together, he'd only talked to Paul, inquiring about the dogs. Had Hammer pulled through, did the team make it back intact? Was Striker putting on weight?

Although his concern for the animals was commendable, he could have asked about her. But, no. Not even once.

Had he had time to think and evaluate their relationship?

Kat snorted. What relationship? So they'd spent time together on the Iditarod. So, they'd both been through a lot, being shot at a few times and attacked by a moose. So, they'd made love during a blizzard. Crazy times made people do things they later regretted.

Vic stepped in first, a grin practically splitting his face in two. "Look what I found at the airport." He moved aside to allow the guests to enter.

"Hi, sweetie." Tazer strode across the room and pressed her cheek to Kat's. "You're looking a little flushed. Are you feeling well, or are you all hot and bothered?"

Kat's face flamed like a gasoline-lit bonfire. "What happened to the subtle Tazer we all knew and loved?"

"Must be the Alaskan air. Brings out the uncouth beast in me." She shed her black trench coat, revealing a go-to-hell-red dress that hugged her perfect figure.

Vic's eyes widened. "Good thing she didn't take off the coat in the car. I would have wrecked for sure."

Paul whistled. "Now, that's what I call a dress."

Kat wanted to throw something at her brother, right after she crawled under a rock. How could she compete with the likes of Tazer when the blond bombshell wore dresses that left very little to the imagination?

Not that Kat was competing. If Sam had been interested, he'd have called.

The man foremost in her thoughts cleared the threshold, setting a suitcase on the wood flooring.

Paul strode toward Sam, a grin spreading across his face. "Good to see you, Sam. How's the arm?"

"Stiff, but getting better. I should regain full use of it in a couple months."

"That's good. I'd hate to think of you giving up your job because of it. The place has been lonely without you." Paul held out a hand.

Sam reached up slowly, shaking Paul's and wincing as he did so. "I'm sorry to say, it's going to continue being lonely without me."

"What's this? I can't believe they'd fire you after Blalock resigned from his position in the Senate."

"How'd that go?" Kat stepped forward, squashing the rise of butterflies in her belly. This was Sam. She shouldn't feel shy and awkward around him.

"It appears Bradley English wasn't the only man Blalock hired to change my mind about my findings. Warren and Al Fendley were in it up to their eyeballs. When Bradley killed Al, Warren came forward and spilled everything he knew about Blalock."

"Wow." Kat's stomach clenched. "Blalock really wanted you out, didn't he?"

"Yes, indeed. Apparently, he had an entire real-estate development planned for the interior where he owned several thousand acres." Sam shed his jacket, hanging it on the coatrack beside the door. "That and some of those acres were the ones he wanted drilled for oil. Not only would he have built a new housing market, but he'd have made a pile of money on the mineral rights." He moved into the living room, his gaze fixed on Kat, unflinching and penetrating.

Moving to position herself on the other side of a leather chair, Kat hoped to hide her wobbly knees. "What's going to happen to Blalock now?"

"He's been offered a deal to disappear and remain silent about the S.O.S. organization."

Kat's brows dipped. "Do you trust him to keep his mouth shut?"

Sam's mouth pressed into a thin line. "Royce gave him incentive. I have no doubt Blalock will take the secret to his grave."

A shiver ran down Kat's body. Royce was loyal and supported his agents fully. But he didn't make it to the top of his profession by being a nice guy. When the need called for it, he could be as ruthless as the rest of them.

Paul clapped a hand to Sam's back. "Then what do you mean you aren't coming back to live here? You know you're always welcome. You're family."

Sam's gaze locked with Kat's. "I don't work for the state of Alaska anymore."

"So they really did fire you?" Paul shook his head. "That's lousy."

"No. I resigned."

"Why?" Kat and Paul asked the question at the same time.

Tazer laughed. "Don't be so shocked. The man couldn't stay away from us." She draped an arm across Kat's shoulder.

"What do you mean?" A kernel of hope rooted in her belly. "Do you have another job?"

"Yes." Again, he pinned her with that intense stare. "I'm going to be working for Royce."

Blood drained from Kat's head and she swayed. Somehow she forced words past her stiff lips. "That's great. I'm sure Royce will be happy to have you back." Then before she made a complete fool of herself, she turned. "I have to check on the bread in the oven. Excuse me, please."

She ran for the kitchen.

"She's been working on dinner all day," Vic said as Kat scurried away.

"I admit, I'm scared. She never cooks." Paul's laughter carried all the way to the kitchen.

Kat's cheeks burned. *Thanks, Paul, for your vote of confidence.* She cooked. Sometimes. Well, okay, Vic did most of the cooking. So what was so wrong with wanting to provide her guests with a decent meal?

Going through the motions of pulling the bread rolls from the oven, she tried to think. But her thoughts were in complete disarray, all swirling around one important issue.

Sam was going to work with the agency in D.C.

Kat almost laughed out loud. She'd just worked a deal with Royce to work out of Alaska. Being home had made her realize just how much she missed it. Or had she hoped to be around Sam more by moving back?

Either way, she'd made her bed. Now she had to lie in it. Alone.

Kat placed the pan of rolls on a trivet, removed her oven mitt and tossed it on the counter.

A sound behind her made her spin, knocking her hand into the hot pan.

"Ouch!"

Callused hands reached out to grab her hand and pull her toward the sink.

"You really should be more careful."

Those knees that were already weak…well, they gave out. Kat leaned back against Sam's solid chest for support, inhaling the scent of his aftershave.

He turned on the faucet and ran her hand under cold water for a minute. While his one hand held hers under the water, the other circled her waist and pulled her to him.

Kat's pulse raced, her breathing became shallow, almost nonexistent. What did he want from her? What did she want from him?

When he finally shut off the water, he turned her in his arms and lifted her burned hand to his lips, pressing a kiss to the reddening welt.

"Are you ready to talk?" he asked, his gaze a sea-foam green, his lips trailing across her fingertips.

"About what?"

"You and me." He sucked one of her fingers between his lips.

Kat's eyes closed at the hail of sensations that one finger was generating. "*Is* there a you and me?"

"I don't know, you tell me."

"You're going to work in D.C. I just made a deal with Royce to work out of Alaska." Her words came out in a rush as a cascade of tremors coursed south. She couldn't think past what he was doing to her fingers and what he could be doing to the rest of her. "Please stop." Her entreaty held no conviction.

"Doesn't Royce tell you anything?" Sam's lips moved from her finger to the inside of her wrist.

"About what?" If he moved any farther up her arm, she'd melt.

"He didn't like the idea of only one agent in the Northwest. I've been assigned to the new Anchorage branch of the S.O.S."

Kat's eyes widened, hope blossoming in her chest. "You have?"

"Seeing as we're partners, it might work better to be collocated." His hands circled behind her and he pulled her hips against his. "Are you up for the challenge?"

Kat stared into his eyes for a moment and then flung her arms around his neck. "Yes!"

Sam spun her around before setting her back on her feet. "Before you get too excited, you have to remember, this is a dangerous job. I might be killed."

"I'll take my chances." She kissed his lips. "If there's one thing I've learned from you, you can't live in the past and you can't worry about the future. You have to live every day like it's your last." She laced her fingers around his neck and pulled him down to her lips. "I can do that, as long as it's with you."

"Good. Now that we have that settled, we have our first mission starting tomorrow."

"We do?" She melted against him, loving the feel of their bodies fitting together.

"The plane will be waiting at the Anchorage airport in the morning." He kissed her lips and trailed a line of kisses along her jawline to her earlobe. "We're flying to Nepal to find an American selling government secrets to the Chinese."

"Um…" Her head dropped back, giving him better access to her neck. "Guess we better get to bed, if we have to get up early in the morning."

"For once we agree." Sam claimed her lips in a full assault on her senses.

Kat settled in for the long haul. This partner thing had its benefits and she planned to explore each and every one of them.

* * * * *

Turn the page for a sneak preview
of the first book in the new miniseries
DIAMONDS DOWN UNDER
from Silhouette Desire®,
VOWS & A VENGEFUL GROOM
by Bronwyn Jameson.

Available January 2008.
(SD #1843)

Silhouette Desire®
Always Powerful, Passionate and Provocative.

Kimberley Blackstone didn't notice the waiting horde of media until it was too late. Flashbulbs exploded around her like a New Year's light show. She skidded to a halt, so abruptly her trailing suitcase all but overtook her.

This had to be a case of mistaken identity. Surely. Kimberley hadn't been on the paparazzi hit list for close to a decade, not since she'd estranged herself from her billionaire father and his headline-hungry diamond business.

But, no, it was *her* name they called. *Her* face was the focus of a swarm of lenses that circled her like avid hornets. Her heart started to pound with fear-fueled adrenaline.

What did they want?

What was going on?

With a rising sense of bewilderment she scanned the crowd for a clue, and her gaze fastened on a tall, leonine figure forcing his way to the front. A tall, familiar figure. Her head came up in stunned recognition, and their gazes collided across the sea of heads before the cameras erupted with another barrage of flashes, this time right in her exposed face.

Blinded by the flashbulbs—and by the shock of that momentary eye-meet—Kimberley didn't realize his intent until he'd forged his way to her side, possibly by the sheer strength of his persomif-nality. She felt his arm wrap around her shoulder, pulling her into the protective shelter of his body, allowing her no time to object. No chance to lift her hands to ward him off.

In the space of a hastily drawn breath, she found herself plastered knee-to-nose against six feet two inches of hard-bodied male.

Ric Perrini.

Her lover for ten torrid weeks, her husband for ten tumultuous days.

Her ex for ten tranquil years.

After all this time, he should not have felt so familiar but, oh dear, he did. She knew the scent of that body and its lean, muscular strength. She knew its heat and its slick power and every response it could draw from hers.

She also recognized the ease with which he'd taken control of the moment and the decisiveness of his deep voice when it rumbled close to her ear. "I have a car waiting outside. Is this your only luggage?"

Kimberley nodded. "I assume you will tell me," she said tightly, "what this welcome party is all about."

"Not while the welcome party is within earshot. No."

Barking a request for the cameramen to stand aside, Perrini took her hand and pulled her into step with his ground-eating stride. Kimberley let him, because he was right, damn his arrogant, Italian-suited hide. Despite the speed with which he whisked her across the airport terminal, she could almost feel the hot breath of the pursuing media on her back.

This was neither the time nor the place for explanations. Inside his car, however, she would get answers.

Now that the initial shock had been blown away— by the haste of their retreat, by the heat of her gathering indignation, by the rush of adrenaline fired by Perrini's presence and the looming verbal battle—her brain was starting to tick over. This had to be her father's doing. And if it was a Howard Blackstone publicity ploy, then it had to be about Blackstone Diamonds, the company that ruled his life.

The knowledge made her chest tighten with a familiar ache of disillusionment.

She'd known her father would be flying in from Sydney for today's opening of the newest in his chain of exclusive, high-end jewelry boutiques. The opulent shopfront sat adjacent to the rival business where Kimberley worked. No coincidence, she thought bitterly, just as it was no coincidence that Ric Perrini was here in Auckland ushering her to his car.

Perrini was Howard Blackstone's right-hand man,

second in command at Blackstone Diamonds, a legacy of his short-lived marriage to the boss's daughter. No doubt her father had sent him to fetch her; the question was *why?*

* * * * *

Get swept away down under with the glitz and glamour of the Blackstone empire as Kimberley tries to determine the real reason behind her "reunion" with Ric....

Look for VOWS & A VENGEFUL GROOM by Bronwyn Jameson, in stores January 2008.

Silhouette® Desire

When Kimberley Blackstone's father is
presumed dead, Kimberley is required to take
over the helm of Blackstone Diamonds. She
has to work closely with her ex, Ric Perrini, to
battle not only the press, but also the fierce
attraction still sizzling between them. Does Ric
feel the same...or is it the power her share of
Blackstone Diamonds will provide him as he
battles for boardroom supremacy.

Look for

VOWS &
A VENGEFUL GROOM

by

BRONWYN
JAMESON

Available January wherever you buy books

REQUEST YOUR FREE BOOKS!

2 FREE NOVELS PLUS 2 FREE GIFTS!

◆ HARLEQUIN®
INTRIGUE®

Breathtaking Romantic Suspense

YES! Please send me 2 FREE Harlequin Intrigue® novels and my 2 FREE gifts. After receiving them, if I don't wish to receive any more books, I can return the shipping statement marked "cancel." If I don't cancel, I will receive 6 brand-new novels every month and be billed just $4.24 per book in the U.S., or $4.99 per book in Canada, plus 25¢ shipping and handling per book and applicable taxes, if any*. That's a savings of close to 15% off the cover price! I understand that accepting the 2 free books and gifts places me under no obligation to buy anything. I can always return a shipment and cancel at any time. Even if I never buy another book from Harlequin, the two free books and gifts are mine to keep forever.

182 HDN EEZ7   382 HDN EEZK

Name	(PLEASE PRINT)	
Address		Apt. #
City	State/Prov.	Zip/Postal Code

Signature (if under 18, a parent or guardian must sign)

Mail to the **Harlequin Reader Service®**:
IN U.S.A.: P.O. Box 1867, Buffalo, NY 14240-1867
IN CANADA: P.O. Box 609, Fort Erie, Ontario L2A 5X3

Not valid to current Harlequin Intrigue subscribers.

Want to try two free books from another line?
Call 1-800-873-8635 or visit www.morefreebooks.com.

* Terms and prices subject to change without notice. NY residents add applicable sales tax. Canadian residents will be charged applicable provincial taxes and GST. This offer is limited to one order per household. All orders subject to approval. Credit or debit balances in a customer's account(s) may be offset by any other outstanding balance owed by or to the customer. Please allow 4 to 6 weeks for delivery.

Your Privacy: Harlequin is committed to protecting your privacy. Our Privacy Policy is available online at www.eHarlequin.com or upon request from the Reader Service. From time to time we make our lists of customers available to reputable firms who may have a product or service of interest to you. If you would prefer we not share your name and address, please check here. ☐

HI07

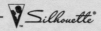

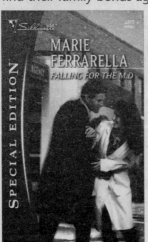

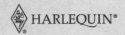